'Did you love me, Nick?'

He met her gaze for a moment then looked down, and his voice was flat when he answered. 'Yes, I loved you, Abbie. But that was a long time ago now, wasn't it?'

He looked up as the others arrived, responding pleasantly to something Sam said. Abbie didn't hear what it was. She couldn't seem to think straight, let alone join in with the conversation. Nick had been right. It had been a long time ago, but it didn't stop her wishing that things might have turned out differently for them...

D1331732

Dear Reader

One of the joys of writing is the opportunity it gives you to create new characters, so you can imagine my delight when I was asked to create a whole town!

Yewdale is purely the product of my imagination but during the course of writing this series the characters who live there became very real to me. Gruff old Isaac Shepherd, nosy Marion Rimmer, the Jackson family with their frequent crises...I would sit down at the typewriter each morning, eager to discover what was happening in their lives.

Writing this series has been quite simply a delight. I have had the pleasure of not only bringing together each couple and watching them fall in love, but of seeing how their lives were enriched by the people around them. I hope that you enjoy reading the books as much as I have enjoyed writing them.

My very best wishes to you.

Jennifer Taylor

Recent Medical Romance™ titles by the same author:

HOME AT LAST
OUR NEW MUMMY
MARRYING HER PARTNER
TAKE ONE BACHELOR

Mills & Boon Enchanted® titles
DESERT MOON
TIDES OF LOVE
ENTICED

THE HUSBAND
SHE NEEDS

BY
JENNIFER TAYLOR

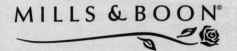

MILLS & BOON®

MILLS & BOON and MILLS & BOON with the Rose Device are registered trademarks of the publisher.

First published in Great Britain 1999
Harlequin Mills & Boon Limited,
Eton House, 18-24 Paradise Road, Richmond, Surrey TW9 1SR

© Jennifer Taylor 1999

ISBN 0 263 81764 4

Set in Times Roman 10½ on 11½ pt.
03-9908-56923-D

Printed and bound in Spain
by Litografia Rosés S.A., Barcelona

CHAPTER ONE

'WELL, time I was on my way, folks,' Abbie Fraser, district nurse for the small Cumbrian town of Yewdale, picked up her case and headed for the staffroom door.

'I did ask you to call on Jack Marsh and change the dressing on his leg, didn't I?' Dr David Ross, one of the three partners in the busy rural practice, called after her, and Abbie paused.

'Yes, I'm going there this afternoon. That ulcer has taken ages to clear up but it's on the mend now,' she assured him.

'And you've got Isaac Shepherd down for a visit?' James Sinclair, another of the partners, queried as he got up to wash his cup. It was a few minutes before morning surgery began and they'd been snatching a break before any patients arrived. 'I saw his son, Frank, yesterday and he's worried that old Isaac is doing too much now he's unable to help him around the farm. We need to keep an eye on him.'

'It will be a while before Frank can do any heavy work,' Sam O'Neill, the locum, put in with a frown. 'He doesn't want to go rushing things or he'll do himself more harm than good.'

'Frank was lucky that he got off so lightly,' Abbie replied soberly, thinking back to what had happened a few weeks previously.

There had been an explosion at the local pottery where Frank Shepherd worked, and it was only thanks to Sam's and James's bravery that Frank hadn't been killed. They had put themselves at risk by going into the burning build-

5

ing to rescue him and two young boys who'd been hiding
in there at the time.

'He was,' David agreed. 'Let's hope nothing like that
ever happens again, although I must say that it's an ill wind
that blows no good.'

'Meaning what?' Abbie asked before anyone else could.

'Oh, only that, thanks to our two heroes here, we now
have a sponsor for the video link,' he explained with a grin.
'The owners of the pottery have offered to pay for the
equipment *and* cover the first year's running costs as a
small token of gratitude for what they did.'

'Really? Why, that's brilliant news!' James's delight was
obvious. It had been his idea to install the new state-of-the-
art computer system which would link them to the local
hospital, but lack of finance had been holding things up for
some time. Abbie was as thrilled as everyone else by the
news.

'That's absolutely marvellous! When is it being delivered?' she demanded.

David laughed. 'I'll get onto the suppliers this morning.
It should be here before the end of the month.'

'Then we'll have to do something to mark the occa-
sion—hold some kind of ceremony to launch it,' she declared, looking at the others for confirmation.

Sam grinned. 'You mean something along the lines of
"God bless this computer and all who surf the Internet"?
Well, I'm game so long as it means cracking open the
champagne.'

'There's been more champagne opened in this surgery in
the past few months than anywhere else in the country!'
Abbie retorted. 'What's the score so far? One wedding, two
engagements and a baby on the way? We should put this
computer to good use and set up a dating agency!'

Everyone laughed as she opened the door. 'Anyway, give
it some thought, you lot. It might be an idea to hold an

open evening to show people what the computer can do. And now I'll love you and leave you. It's time I headed for the hills.'

She was still smiling as she hurried out to her car. It was a windy day in late October and clouds were scudding across the sky above the peaks of the surrounding mountains. Rain was forecast for later but there was no sign of it as yet.

She paused before getting into her car to sniff appreciatively at the spicy scents of autumn carried on the breeze. Coming back to Yewdale to live and work after her divorce—it had been the right decision. She'd found what she'd been looking for here—a job she loved and people who cared about her. It had helped her get over the heartache...

'Hang on a minute, Abbie.'

She glanced round as someone called her. Planting her hands on her shapely hips, she glared at the woman hurrying towards her. 'I've got a list as long as my arm already so I hope you aren't thinking of adding anyone else to it, Elizabeth Allen, or I might just hand in my notice.'

'You know you love being busy,' Elizabeth replied with a grin. She was the third partner in the practice and she and Abbie were firm friends as well as colleagues. She knew very well that Abbie was teasing. 'Anyway, it should only be a quick call. Do you think you can *squeeze* it in?'

'I suppose so.' Abbie sighed as she let the car door close. 'Who do you want me to see, then?'

'Major Delaney,' Elizabeth glanced at the card she was holding, missing the start Abbie gave. 'His blood pressure was extremely high when I saw him last week so I had to prescribe something stronger than the diuretic he'd been taking. It should do the trick but I'd like you to call in and see how he is today just to be on the safe side.'

'I imagine the stress he's been under recently hasn't helped,' she said quietly.

'I'm sure it hasn't.' Elizabeth sighed. 'It's such a shame about his son, isn't it? Nick's what…thirty? Being confined to a wheelchair at his age must be hard for him and his family to come to terms with.'

'He's thirty-three.' Abbie coloured as she saw Elizabeth look at her. She avoided her eyes as she took the card and tucked it into her case.

'Of course. He's almost the same age as you, isn't he? I'd forgotten that you and Nick virtually grew up together. Your mother was the Delaneys' housekeeper, wasn't she?'

'That's right. But Nick was away at school most of the time,' she said quickly. Talking about Nick Delaney—that wasn't easy even now and she was sorry that she'd brought the subject up. 'We didn't see that much of each other really.'

'I suppose not…' Elizabeth glanced round as James shouted to tell her there was a phone call for her. 'I'll have to go. I'll see you later, then. Oh, and if you see Nick, give him my regards, will you?'

'He's at home?' She couldn't keep the surprise from her voice and she saw Elizabeth frown.

'Didn't you know? The hospital discharged him over a week ago and he's staying at the house. I imagine he'll be pleased to see you, Abbie. At a time like this Nick needs his friends around him, doesn't he?'

She was gone before Abbie could say anything, not that there was much she could think of to say. She quickly got into her car and left the surgery. Several of the calls she had to make entailed long drives to get to them so she couldn't afford to waste any more time. However, her mind was less on the logistics of fitting twelve hours' work into an eight-hour day than on the conversation she'd just had.

Nick Delaney was home. She hadn't considered the possibility that he might come back to Yewdale and she wasn't sure how it made her feel to know that he was here. Not that it mattered, of course. She and Nick might have been friends once but she doubted if he thought of her as that now. Nick had made it plain some time ago that she had no place in his life!

She sighed as she realised that she'd been so preoccupied that she'd driven into town, instead of taking the road out to her first call at one of the outlying farms. It seemed silly to turn round and go all the way back. She'd go straight to the Delaneys' house and get that over with, then catch up with the rest of her calls as planned.

It took only a few minutes to reach the imposing stone house set in its own grounds on the outskirts of the town. Abbie drew up outside the front door then sat for a moment as the memories came flooding back. Her mother had worked for the Delaneys for many years until her retirement and Abbie had spent a lot of time at the house. She'd told Elizabeth that she hadn't seen much of Nick because he'd been away at school but that hadn't been quite true.

During the holidays they'd spent all their time together. Nick had been the big brother she'd never had, the best friend she'd confided in, the one person she'd trusted and believed in completely until everything had changed when she was eighteen. Nothing had been the same after that summer.

There was a hint of sadness in her dove-grey eyes as she got out of the car but not for the life of her would she have let anyone know how on edge she felt as she rang the old-fashioned bell. Mrs Delaney herself opened the door and she smiled as she saw her.

'Come in, my dear. I expect you've come to see the Major. Dr Allen said that she'd ask you to call. He's in the conservatory, I think. You know the way so would you mind if I don't come with you?' She glanced at the phone.

'I was just about to make a call and if I don't do it now I'll forget!'

'Of course not,' Abbie replied with a smile as she headed across the hall. She knew the layout of the house so well that she didn't need to be shown the way. The conservatory was built onto the back of the house, a flower-filled bower which overlooked the rear gardens. Major Delaney's hobby was growing orchids and he spent a lot of his time there, attending to their needs.

Closing the door carefully behind her, she made her way along the tiled path between the beds of brilliant blooms. The heat was intense, the air humid with the moisture the flowers needed to flourish. The thick foliage made it impossible to see very far, but she guessed that Major Delaney would be sitting in his favourite spot in the centre of this tropical paradise so she headed straight there and wasn't surprised when she spotted the back of his head.

'Good morning, and how are you today…?' she began, then felt her heart lurch painfully as the man looked round and she realised that it wasn't Major Delaney at all but Nick. In a fast sweep her shocked gaze took in the changes that had occurred since they had last met.

His thick dark brown hair had flecks of silver now, although his brows and lashes were still as sooty as ever. His face was deeply lined, the shadows under his dark blue eyes lending a brooding intensity to his gaze as he stared at her. It was Nick but not as she remembered him, and Abbie felt unexpected tears burn her eyes. No matter what had happened between them she would never have wished this on him!

'Well, well, if it isn't Abbie. To what do I owe this honour, I wonder?'

His voice seemed to have changed as well, sounding harsher to her ears. Abbie's hands clenched as she struggled to contain the rush of emotions which had caught her totally unprepared. 'I came to see your father, actually. Your mother said he was in here.'

'I see. So this isn't a social call but a professional one. I should have realised.' He smiled but there was no hint of warmth in his eyes as they moved deliberately from the top of her glossy red-brown curls to the tips of her sensible black shoes. 'You're looking well, Abbie. How's life been treating you, then? Better than it's treated me, obviously.'

He gave a discordant laugh as he saw her struggle for something to say. 'No, don't! Please. I don't want to hear any more platitudes or be reminded how lucky I am. I don't feel lucky if you want the truth. But, then, I don't imagine you want to hear that because it makes you uncomfortable, doesn't it? Poor Nick Delaney, did you know he's been crippled? Still, at least he wasn't killed and that's something to be thankful for, isn't it?'

Abbie took a deep breath but it did little to control the shock she felt at his bitter mockery. Maybe it was to be expected after what had happened to him but this wasn't the way the Nick she'd known would have reacted. 'Yes, it is something to be thankful for. At least you're here and obviously your mind hasn't been affected in any way. But if you don't want to hear any platitudes then that's fine by me, Nick. You just sit there and feel sorry for yourself. Seems to me that you're making a first-rate job of it!'

She swung round to leave, wondering sickly why she'd said such an awful thing. How would she have felt if she'd found herself in the same situation? She was just debating whether she should apologise when he spoke.

'At least I'm still good at something, then.'

There was a touch of dry humour in his voice now, a hint of wryness in his eyes as she turned to look at him. He shrugged, his mouth twisting into a thin smile. 'I should have known that the last person I'd get sympathy from would be you, Abbie Fraser!'

'If I thought you really needed it...' She gave him a tentative smile in return, her heart aching as he spun the wheelchair round so that they were facing one another. She couldn't stop her gaze from dropping to his rug-covered legs and she heard him take a deep breath.

'Several fractured vertebrae, ruptured ligaments and severe bruising to the spinal cord,' he recited tonelessly.

'And the prognosis?' It was hard to keep her tone as devoid of emotion as his was, but she tried her best.

'A twenty–eighty chance that I might recover some movement in my legs in the next twelve months.' He shrugged. 'I think the odds they quoted were a bit optimistic.'

'The doctors wouldn't have told you that if they didn't believe it, Nick,' she countered. 'What point would there be in raising your hopes?'

'I'd hardly call it raising my hopes!' He laughed harshly. 'Not when there's an eighty per cent chance that I'll be stuck in this thing for the rest of my days.'

She hated to hear him sound so...so defeated. Straightening her shoulders, she stared at him. 'So, what do you intend to do about it?'

'What do you suggest?' His dark brows rose mockingly. 'I'm hardly in a position to do very much, I'd say.'

'There's physiotherapy. You know as well as I do that keeping your muscles supple to prevent them wasting could improve your chances of regaining your mobility.'

'Think so? The damage to the spinal cord was extensive. There's very little hope that I'll recover any movement in my legs,' he stated baldly, staring at her with hard blue eyes.

'So that means you aren't even going to try?' she challenged. 'What's the matter, Nick? Aren't you willing to take a chance any more?'

'Not if it means living under a false illusion.' His smile

was cynical. 'Surely you understand that, Abbie? You were the one who always wanted everything to come with a guarantee.'

He threw the taunt back at her in the most painful way possible and she turned away so that he couldn't see how it hurt. It had been her refusal to take a risk which had caused the rift between them, and to have Nick use that against her now hurt more than it should have done. It was also an indication of how much he'd changed. The Nick she remembered would never have willingly tried to hurt her.

'Obviously, it's up to you what you decide to do,' she said in a stiff little voice. 'I'd better go and find your father. I've a lot of calls to do...'

'I'm sorry.' The apology was so curt that for a moment she wondered if she'd heard it correctly. She glanced round as he rolled the wheelchair over to her. His face was set as he looked up at her yet there was something about the expression in his deep blue eyes which spoke of real regret. 'I shouldn't take my frustrations out on you, Abbie.'

'No, you shouldn't, but it's understandable.' She took a quick breath but it did little to contain the pain she felt. He might have changed outwardly but when he looked at her like that there was a trace of the old Nick she remembered, which tugged at her heartstrings painfully.

'It must be hard, Nick,' she said softly, watching his face so that she saw the myriad emotions which crossed it in rapid succession.

'It is.' He looked away and his voice was once more devoid of expression. 'But I'm just going to have to learn to accept it, aren't I? It was nice seeing you again, Abbie. Take care.'

He swung the chair round and headed for the door leading to the terrace. It must have been difficult, opening it, but she made herself stay where she was rather than offering to help because she sensed that Nick would resent it. He'd always had a stubborn streak, always been determined to achieve whatever he'd set out to. It had stood him in good stead over the years, as she knew, because word of his achievements had carried back to Yewdale even though he'd rarely visited the town.

Nick Delaney was one of the country's most highly respected psychiatrists now. As well as working at a top London teaching hospital, he was much in demand to lecture around the world. It had taken hard work *and* determination to get to this point at such a young age, and it made his present attitude all the more difficult to understand.

Why wasn't Nick fighting this, as she'd have expected him to? she wondered as she made her way back into the house. It was very strange.

Abbie finally tracked down Major Delaney to his study, where he was reading the morning papers. A man in his mid-sixties, he still bore the stamp of his military training in his upright bearing. He looked round when Abbie entered the room and smiled at her.

'Ah, no rest for the wicked, eh? Did Dr Allen send you, my dear?'

'That's right,' Abbie replied as she put her bag down on a side table and took out her sphygmomanometer. 'She wants me to check your blood pressure again to see if the new medication is having the desired effect.'

He grunted. 'Well, I suppose I'd better let you get on with it, but it does seem like a lot of fuss over nothing to me.' The major slipped off his old tweed jacket then impatiently rolled up his shirtsleeve. 'Of course it was Pamela who insisted I go and see the doctor in the first place. Far as I was concerned, everything was hunky-dory!'

'Now, Ronald, you know very well that you've been having dizzy spells lately.' Mrs Delaney came into the room at that moment. 'And that isn't a good sign, as Dr Allen told you.'

'It certainly isn't,' Abbie agreed. She wrapped the cuff round the major's arm and inflated it, carefully taking note of the reading. 'Well, you'll be pleased to know that it's much better than it was. Obviously, the new tablets are doing their job. I'll let Dr Allen know when I get back to the surgery. I'm sure you know what I'm going to say, Major, but I'll say it anyway—avoid too much dairy produce, keep any alcohol to a minimum and, if you're still smoking that pipe, you really must think about giving it up.'

'At this rate there'll be nothing left worth living for!' Major Delaney retorted, sounding decidedly put out as he slipped his jacket back on.

'Take no notice, my dear. Ronald's trouble is that he is so used to giving orders that he hates taking them!' Mrs Delaney laughed affectionately as she led the way from the room. She closed the door but, instead of ushering Abbie to the front door, took her into the small sitting-room across the hall. 'I know how busy you must be but I wanted a word with you about Nick. You saw him just now, I imagine?'

'I did.' She struggled to find something diplomatic to say but Mrs Delaney shook her head.

'No, don't bother, my dear. I know what you're thinking and you're right. Nick isn't handling this as any of us might have expected him to, is he?'

'He seems very…well, bitter is the only word I can come up with,' Abbie replied with a frown. 'Although maybe that's to be expected. He must have been devastated by the prognosis.'

'I'm sure he was…*is*. We all are.' Pamela Delaney sighed sadly, unable to hide her pain at what had happened to her only son. 'Why did it have to be Nick of all people?

All he's ever done is try to help others. It doesn't seem fair!'

'It doesn't. But it's happened and, hard though it may be, Nick has to deal with it. Yet he gives the impression that he doesn't want to fight any more. I can't understand it because it isn't like him,' she declared, then coloured as the older woman laughed softly at the passion in her voice.

'You and Nick were always such good friends, my dear. I remember you two spending all your time together during the school holidays. Several times Nick was invited to stay with some friend or other but he always refused because he wanted to come back home to see you.'

Abbie had to clear her throat. She'd never realised that before. 'I enjoyed being with him,' she said huskily. 'We just seemed to understand one another so well when we were children.'

'Maybe you still do understand one another?' Mrs Delaney said softly. 'Oh, Nick has lots of friends but I don't think there's ever been anyone he confided in like he confided in you. It makes me feel less guilty about what I'm going to ask you, Abbie—will you try to help Nick see that he still has a future? Nobody else seems to be able to get through to him and it breaks my heart to think that he's given up.'

'I... Of course, but I'm not sure that Nick would want my help.' She looked away, not wanting Mrs Delaney to see the pain in her eyes as she thought about their recent encounter.

'I'm sure he doesn't!' Mrs Delaney laughed when she saw her surprise. 'Nick is determined that he doesn't want *anyone's* help. But I'm sure I can leave it to you to find a way round that. If anyone can make that stubborn boy of mine see sense then it's you, Abbie, because you know him so well!'

Mrs Delaney led the way from the room, obviously considering the conversation over now that she'd achieved her objective. Abbie got into her car and waved before she drove away. She paused at the gates and glanced back, her heart turning over as she saw the wheelchair parked on the terrace behind the house.

Nick was staring towards the mountains in the distance and didn't appear to have noticed her. The wind had blown his hair back and his face bore the hallmarks of pain and disillusionment. Suddenly Abbie knew that his mother had been wrong. Once she might have known Nick Delaney as well as she'd known herself, but not any longer. The man sitting in that chair was a stranger to her so how could she help him?

She pulled out into the road and her heart was heavy as she set off to her next call. The Nick Delaney she had once known and loved was gone for ever. It felt as though something precious inside her had been lost.

CHAPTER TWO

It was a busy day and Abbie was glad when she arrived at her last call, which was at Isaac Shepherd's farm. The old man had suffered a heart attack some months previously and it was a testament both to the nursing skill he'd received and his own gritty determination that he was leading an active life once again.

'Well, everything appears to be fine, Mr Shepherd. Your blood pressure is excellent and you haven't had any other problems, I take it?' Abbie rolled up her stethoscope and packed it away in her case as she finished the check-up.

'Feel fit as a fiddle. No need to go worrying about me, lass,' Isaac assured her, rolling down his sleeve. He walked her out to her car, screwing up his eyes as he gazed at the sky. 'Storm's coming, from the look of it. You want to hurry up and get yourself off home. Going to be a bad 'un.'

Abbie glanced at the lowering clouds. Even in the short time she'd been at the farm the weather had changed dramatically. 'The forecast said to expect rain.'

'Aye, and it was right for once,' Isaac agreed with all the disdain of a countryman who'd never needed to listen to a forecast.

Abbie laughed as she got into her car. 'Well, I'll see you in a month's time, Mr Shepherd. Take care, now. I know you're feeling fit but don't overdo things.'

'Oh, I won't. I've just taken on young Billy Murray to give me a hand. Lad needed work now he's got responsibilities and, what with my Frank still laid up, I was finding it hard to manage. Seemed like the best solution all round.'

'Sounds like a great idea to me,' she agreed as she started

the engine. 'I bet Billy was pleased, and it will set Frank's mind at rest, knowing that you aren't trying to do everything yourself.'

'That's what I thought,' Issac said laconically as he waved her off.

She headed back to town, thinking how well things were working out. Billy Murray was about to become a father so he needed the money the job would bring in. He was only seventeen and his parents had taken the news very badly, but he was a steady, reliable boy who would work hard. It would be a big weight off Frank's mind, too, knowing that his father had help on the farm.

In fact, situations were rarely as black as they first appeared, although she doubted that Nick would agree with that sentiment.

She sighed as she realised that once again her thoughts were back with him. Try as she may, she couldn't help thinking about what had happened that morning. Maybe Nick *was* virtually a stranger to her now, but surely there was something she could do to help him?

The thought kept her busy as she drove back to town. The storm broke when she still had a couple of miles to go, the wind lashing rain against the windscreen so that it was difficult to see out. It was pure good luck that she happened to spot the woman struggling along the road on foot and realised that it was Mrs Delaney.

She pulled up alongside and leant over to open the door. 'Want a lift?'

'Oh, what a lifesaver you are!' Mrs Delaney climbed gratefully into the car. She settled the basket of blackberries on her knee with a rueful laugh. 'I should have started back as soon as I saw the clouds gathering but I was doing so well that I hated to call it a day!'

Abbie smiled as she looked at the heap of plump berries.

'Well, from the look of it, you should have plenty of fruit there to keep you busy. Are you making jam?'

'Yes. Nick always loved my blackberry jam so I thought it would be a treat for him. This is kind of you, my dear. I do hope I'm not taking you out of your way.'

'No, I was on my way home anyway,' she assured her quickly, turning into the Delaneys' drive and pulling up outside the door for the second time that day.

'In that case you must come in and have a cup of tea.' Mrs Delaney held up her hand when Abbie started to protest. 'No, I insist. Come along, now.'

She hurried out of the car, leaving Abbie little option but to follow her. 'Go on through to the small sitting-room while I see about that tea,' Mrs Delaney instructed, before disappearing down the hall towards the kitchen.

Abbie sighed as she did as she was told. She wasn't sure it was a good idea to risk bumping into Nick again so soon. She would have liked more time to have got her thoughts in some kind of order before she saw him again. However, it seemed she was doomed to disappointment as she opened the sitting-room door and found him in there.

'What are you doing here again?' he demanded, making no attempt to hide his displeasure.

'Well, I didn't come to enjoy your charming company, that's for sure,' she retorted, stung into replying in the same vein. 'I was driving home and spotted your mother. As it was bucketing down, I offered her a lift and she insisted I come in for a cup of tea.'

'Really? How convenient.' He gave her a sardonic smile which didn't quite mask the lines of strain on his face.

'Convenient? I'm sorry but I'm not with you,' Abbie said, wondering if there was something wrong with him. Surely it couldn't be comfortable, sitting bolt upright in the chair the way he was doing?

'Come on, Abbie! It's my legs that are paralysed, not

my brain! Mother had a word with you about me this morning, didn't she? Something along the lines of would you see what you could do to cheer me up?' He laughed harshly as he saw the guilty start she gave. 'Mmm, I thought so. Otherwise you wouldn't be here now, would you? After all, why should you care—?'

He broke off on a gasp, his face turning ashen as the colour drained from it. Abbie could see that his hands were gripping the arms of the chair so hard that his knuckles gleamed whitely through his skin.

'Nick, what is it?' she demanded, going over to kneel down in front of him.

'Muscle spasm…' he grated, his teeth clenching as another wave of pain hit him.

'Where? In your back?' she demanded, sliding her hand down the gap between him and the chair so that she could feel the knot in the muscles just below his waist.

He managed to nod his head, all his attention focused on getting through the pain. Abbie stood up as she came to a swift decision. 'It needs massaging but you'll have to lie down before I can do that properly. Which is your room?'

'The…breakfast-room… It's been converted…' He couldn't manage anything else, his jaw clamping as the pain spasmed through him once more. Abbie didn't waste any more time as she pushed his chair across the hall.

The breakfast-room had rarely been used in the past. Now it had been converted into a functional bedroom with everything arranged on a level which someone in a wheel-chair could cope with. A section had been partitioned off to form an *en suite* bathroom, and once again care had been taken to ensure that the facilities were suitable for someone with limited mobility. However, she was less concerned with the modifications than in doing something to alleviate Nick's discomfort.

'Can you get into the bed by yourself or should I help?'

'I can manage!' he bit out curtly. It must have taken every bit of strength he possessed to lever himself out of the chair, using the grab rail, and get onto the bed, and once he'd managed it, it was obvious that he could do little else. Without bothering to ask this time, Abbie quickly drew the sweater over his head and dealt with his shirt, her fingers working swiftly as she unfastened the tiny pearl buttons.

She slid the shirt off his shoulders, trying to ignore the sudden surge her heart gave as her hands encountered smooth, warm skin. Nick had always tanned easily and his skin was a delicious golden brown even now. The pelt of dark hair covering his chest did little to disguise the power of the muscles in his upper torso which not even his illness had affected.

She took a small breath to contain the rush of awareness she felt as she eased him down on the bed and gently rolled him over so that she could massage the corded muscles in his back. It shocked her that she should feel like this after such a long time. What she'd felt for Nick was in the past but it was impossible not to be aware of him. It was only by focusing her attention on easing his pain that helped her cope.

'How is it feeling now?' she asked softly, her fingers working deep into the knot of muscles in his lower back. There was a red scar line down his spine, evidence of the surgeon's handiwork, and her heart ached as she saw it. It seemed such a small legacy of the accident and gave little indication of the devastation it had caused.

'Better…' He let out a weary sigh. 'It hits you out of the blue sometimes and there's nothing you can do about it—that's the worst thing.'

'What have the doctors said, Nick? Have they given you anything to control the pain?' she queried, her hands still kneading away. He had his face half turned into the pillows, a lock of hair falling across his forehead. His hair was as thick as ever, the odd silvery strands gleaming in the light. Abbie had the craziest urge to brush it back from his forehead just so she could test its crisp vitality…

'Ouch!'

His exclamation brought a rush of heat to her face as she realised that she had dug a little too hard into the relaxing muscles. 'Sorry,' she muttered to cover her confusion.

He brushed the hair back from his face, frowning as he noticed her heightened colour. 'Are you OK, Abbie?'

'I… Yes. It's…it's hard work, doing this, that's all,' she stammered and saw him grimace.

'That's enough, then. It feels a whole lot better—honestly,' he said firmly.

'Just let me make sure the cramp has gone…' Once again she massaged the troublesome spot then jumped when he laid his hand over hers. Abbie knew that he'd only intended to make her stop yet neither of them could have been prepared for the surge of electricity that shot through them both.

She heard Nick take a deep breath as his hand gripped hers for a moment which could have lasted no longer than a millisecond and yet seemed to span an eternity. She had the feeling that time had become elastic, that split second stretching to infinity as Nick's fingers held hers fast. Then abruptly he pushed her hand away and rolled over, levering himself up against the pillows with a speed that brought an immediate protest from her lips.

'Careful! You'll undo all my good work.' She tagged on a laugh which was meant to be light but which failed to hit the right note. 'They say that doctors make the worst patients, and they're right, obviously!'

'I'm not your patient, Abbie.' His voice was harsh all of a sudden, his eyes filled with an anger that stunned her.

'I…I know you're not. I'm sorry, Nick, but what's

wrong?' she asked, unable to understand his swift change of mood. ·

'What's wrong is that I don't need your help either in a personal or a *professional* capacity. So don't waste your time on me, Abbie. I don't need anyone's pity!'

'Oh, don't worry on that score, Nick!' She drew herself up, more hurt than she cared to admit by his rejection. 'I have better things to do than waste my sympathy on someone who doesn't appreciate it. Now, if you'll excuse me, I'll go and see if your mother has made that tea. Although a good stiff whisky would be more welcome! There's nothing like dealing with an arrogant, self-centred, peevish, thirty-three-year-old child to try one's patience to the limit!'

She swung round then came to an abrupt halt as she found Mrs Delaney in the doorway. It was obvious that the older woman must have heard every word but she gave absolutely no sign as she smiled pleasantly at Abbie. 'Tea in the small sitting-room when you're ready, my dear.'

She turned and walked calmly back across the hall without another word. Abbie took a deep breath, wishing she could disappear into the deepest, darkest hole…

She spun round as she heard Nick laugh, her eyes widening as she saw the amusement on his face. 'Only you would come out and say what I'm sure everyone has been thinking, Abbie!'

'Pardon?' she stared at him in confusion and saw his smile fade.

'That everyone has been tiptoeing around me for weeks because they're afraid of upsetting me. I know they mean well but it doesn't help, to be honest. It just makes me feel even more alienated.' He held out his hand and his blue eyes were suddenly serious. 'And it means that I get away with behaving like a complete and utter boor.'

'I guess you've had a genuine excuse for your bad behaviour, although it's probably wearing a bit thin now,' she replied softly. She went over to the bed and put her hand into his, feeling the jolt her pulse gave at the contact. She knew without having to look at Nick that he'd felt the same thing. It made her head spin because it was so unexpected, so…so crazy! She couldn't still feel anything for him after all this time, as he couldn't feel anything for her, and yet there was that devastating flash of awareness each time they touched.

'It probably is.' His voice sounded suddenly deeper and softer than it had done, rubbing sensuously against nerves that were already raw. Abbie struggled to contain the rush of sensations but it wasn't easy with Nick holding her hand.

She tried to draw away but he wouldn't let her go as he looked at her with shadowed blue eyes which held a plea she couldn't ignore. 'Do you think I can do it, Abbie? Do you think I can get through this?'

It almost broke her heart to hear the uncertainty in his voice and see the fear in his eyes. She bent towards him, wanting to make him believe that she was telling the truth—wanting it to *be* true. 'Yes! I know you, Nick. If anyone can rebuild his life then you can.'

'You sound as though you really care what happens to me.' His voice was so low that she wasn't sure if he'd intended her to hear, let alone expected an answer. He let go of her hand abruptly and his eyes were suddenly hooded so that she couldn't tell what he was thinking.

'I do care, Nick,' she said quietly, then realised how very personal that had sounded and hurriedly moderated her reply. 'There are a lot of people who care about you. Now, I'd better go and have that tea *and* try to convince your mother that I don't usually bully my patients.'

'I've already told you that I have no intention of being one of your patients, Abbie.'

'Then what do you want to be?' The words came out

before she could stop them and she felt her heart jolt as she realised what she'd said.

'How about friends? Think it's possible after all this time?' he asked quietly, his eyes suddenly locked to her face.

'Maybe.' It took every scrap of determination to respond lightly, but not for the world would she have let him see how she felt about the suggestion. Surely it was the best thing possible in the circumstances, that they go back to being friends—as they had been for so long? So why did she feel disappointed that was all he wanted from her? It didn't make sense.

She gave an edgy little laugh. 'It depends.'

'On what?' His dark brows knitted into a frown.

'On how well you behave, of course!' She wagged a finger at him. 'You're on trial, Delaney—no more tantrums, no more peevishness and no more lying down and giving up. If you want my friendship you have to earn it!'

She turned and headed out of the door, pausing when Nick said softly, 'You're a hard-hearted woman, Abbie Fraser. I never realised that before.'

She didn't say anything nor did she look back. She didn't dare! Her heart had always been far too soft where Nick was concerned. That was the trouble.

Abbie made herself beans on toast when she got home because she was too tired to bother cooking a meal. She carried the tray into the sitting-room and balanced it on her knee while she watched television as she ate.

Her mother had moved to the south coast the year before, finding the milder temperatures there kinder to her arthritis. Abbie was pleased that she'd settled in so well to her new home and made so many friends, but sometimes she missed her company when she got in at night.

Not that she wasn't used to being on her own. When

she'd been married, Paul had rarely stayed in of a night, preferring to go out with his friends than spend time with her. It had been one of the things they'd rowed about most.

She sighed as she carried the tray back to the kitchen. She tried not to think about her disastrous marriage very often, but recently she'd found her thoughts going back to the two brief years she and Paul had spent together.

Would things have turned out differently if Megan hadn't died? she wondered sadly as she picked up the photograph from the top of the fridge.

She ran a finger gently over her daughter's face, her heart aching as she recalled how soft Megan's skin had been. Megan had been just six months old when she'd died and all Abbie had left were a few pictures and her memories. Sometimes it felt as though she had dreamt the whole thing, and that Megan had never existed.

The telephone suddenly rang and she put the picture down and went to answer it with relief. Thoughts of Megan were always so painful that she tried to avoid them. It was Sam O'Neill on the phone, calling to see if she wanted to go down to the pub for a drink.

'Well, I don't know…' Abbie hedged, not sure if she felt like being sociable that night.

'Oh, come on, why not? It will do you good to get out,' Sam said encouragingly. He and Abbie had been firm friends ever since he'd come to Yewdale to work almost two years before and not even his recent engagement to Holly Ross, David Ross's eldest daughter, had changed that.

'You don't want to think of me sitting there all by myself, drowning my sorrows in a pint, do you?' he wheedled, shamelessly playing on her sympathy.

'What sorrows?' Abbie retorted. 'You've been flying high as a kite since Holly—very foolishly—agreed to marry you, O'Neill!'

'Then is it any wonder I'm down in the dumps because I haven't seen her for two whole weeks?' he demanded, not to be deterred.

Abbie laughed. 'You have an answer for everything! All right, then, I'll come. I'll see you down there in what…half an hour?'

She was still smiling as she ran upstairs to change out of her uniform dress. She took a quick shower then hunted through her wardrobe for something to wear. Considering her initial reluctance, she felt like making an effort that night, although there wasn't going to be anyone there to appreciate it, she realised wryly. A silk shirt in a pearly grey with darker grey trousers seemed to fit the bill and would go nicely under her new black wool jacket.

She dressed quickly then did her face and brushed her reddish-brown hair until it fell in a silky-smooth curve around her face. A light spray of Opium perfume was the finishing touch and she felt quite pleased with her appearance when she stepped back from the mirror. Although she said so herself, she didn't look bad!

The Fleece was fairly empty when she arrived, just a few diehards propping up the bar. She spotted Sam in the far corner and waved, miming to ask him if he wanted a drink. He shook his head as he held up a half-full pint glass so she bought herself a glass of shandy and went to join him.

'So, what sort of a day have you had, then?' he asked, putting his glass down on a coaster.

'Busy, but when isn't it?' Abbie took a sip of shandy and grimaced. 'My lists seem to get longer as each week passes.'

'It's the same in surgery. James was saying that they'd have had to advertise for another locum if I'd gone as planned—' he broke off with a grin. 'Ah, speak of the devil.'

Abbie glanced round and saw James coming towards

them. However, it wasn't the sight of him that made her heart start to drum but the man who was with him. She felt the colour run up her face as she watched Nick Delaney steering his chair between the tables. A few people stopped him *en route* to exchange greetings and she was glad of the delay because it gave her time to get herself in hand. However, she couldn't deny that her heart was racing when he finally stopped by their table.

'I might have known I'd find someone from the surgery here!' James exclaimed, grinning at her and Sam.

'Listen to who's talking!' Sam replied with a laugh. He turned to Nick and held out his hand. 'I'm Sam O'Neill, the locum, by the way.'

'Nick Delaney,' Nick shook his hand then turned to Abbie. 'Hello again.'

'He-hello. How are you feeling now?' she asked softly, more for something to say than anything else. Seeing Nick like this so unexpectedly, it had thrown her into a spin so that she wasn't sure if she was on her head or her heels.

'Fine, thanks. That massage did the trick all right.' He turned as James spoke and Abbie let out the small breath she was holding.

'I had no idea the Nick Delaney I knew was Major Delaney's son until Elizabeth mentioned he was a psychiatrist and I put two and two together,' he explained, pulling out a chair and sitting down. 'I called round to see him tonight and persuaded him to come out for a drink.'

'So you're a psychiatrist?' Sam leant forward, his interest piqued by this piece of information. 'Where do you practise?'

'London.' Nick grimaced. 'Or I did before this happened.'

'I imagine you'll go back to it?' Sam queried.

'Maybe.' Nick deliberately turned the conversation away from himself. 'So, James, how long have you been here in

Yewdale? I did hear on the grapevine that you'd gone into general practice up north but I had no idea that you'd come here.'

'Seven months now. It was the best decision I ever made, too.' James smiled. 'I wouldn't have met Elizabeth otherwise.'

'And you're getting married when?' Nick asked, glancing round as Harry Shaw, the licensee, arrived with their drinks. 'Thanks.'

'You're welcome. Nice to see you out and about, Nick,' Harry replied sincerely, putting the glasses down before going back to the bar.

'December,' James replied, picking up the conversation once more. 'We were due to get married in September but Elizabeth's father had another heart attack so we postponed it. Dr Allen was staying with Elizabeth's sister in Melbourne,' he explained, 'so he wasn't fit to fly home. He should be well enough to make the journey by the end of next month, though.'

'That must have been disappointing,' Nick sympathised. 'Mother told me that Liz was engaged but, like you, I never put two and two together and realised to whom. She was telling me also that David has remarried.'

'That's right.' James grinned. 'And they have a baby on the way. Then Sam here has just got engaged to David's oldest daughter, Holly. They're planning on getting married when she finishes medical school, then going out to Africa to work.'

'Good heavens!' Nick turned to Abbie with a smile still lingering on his lips. 'And how about you, Abbie? Surely you aren't the odd one out around here?'

Abbie picked up her glass, trying not to let him see how the comment stung, although she had no idea why it should. 'What's the saying about once bitten twice shy?'

Her tone was light enough to make the other two laugh

but Nick's eyes darkened. Under cover of the laughter he said softly, 'Was it really that bad?'

She shrugged, trying to make light of the question. 'Divorce is never easy.'

'You had a child, didn't you?' He must have seen her surprise because he explained flatly, 'Mother wrote and told me.'

'I see. Yes, I had a daughter.' Abbie stared down at her glass, unable to explain why she felt an urge to cry. Maybe it was because she'd been thinking about Megan earlier, or maybe it was because Nick had made it plain that unless he'd been force-fed the information he wouldn't have been interested in what had happened to her, but she felt tears gather behind her eyes. 'She died.'

'I had no idea...' There was anguish in his eyes as he looked at her. It seemed the most natural thing in the world when he reached out and took her hand. 'I'm sorry, Abbie. I really didn't know.'

'So am I, Nick.' She gave him a tremulous smile before she removed her hand and picked up her glass. She saw Sam glance at her before he quickly started to talk about how busy they'd been lately.

She was grateful for the change of subject. She found that talking about Megan to Nick was unbearably painful because she was conscious of the fact that Megan could have been *his* daughter if things had been different...

A sudden crash from the direction of the bar captured their attention and they all turned to see what was happening. Abbie frowned as she saw the young man who had dropped a tray full of glasses. 'Isn't that Harry's son, Adrian? I didn't know he was home.'

'He only came back at the weekend,' James informed them. 'He was due to come home a few months ago but they had to re-admit him to hospital. Adrian is schizophrenic,' he added for Nick's benefit.

'Difficult. It's the most common psychotic illness and extremely disabling,' Nick replied. 'The fact that it strikes at a relatively young age is heart-breaking for the patient's family.'

'You've dealt with many schizophrenics in the course of your work, I imagine?' Abbie asked quietly, watching as Harry organised the clearing up of the broken glass.

'Too many, unfortunately. What treatment is Adrian receiving?' he asked.

'He's on haloperidol,' James replied.

'It's effective in controlling a lot of the symptoms—hallucinations, delusions, and so on—but it can have distressing side effects, which is why so many stop taking their medication when they leave hospital,' Nick explained. 'They find it hard to cope with the tremors and abnormal muscle movements once they're mixing with people who don't understand what's wrong.'

'So you remove one social problem and create another?' Sam said thoughtfully.

'That's about it. It's a balance between the possible danger a schizophrenic poses to himself and society and the quality of life he can expect. It's never easy.'

Nick spoke with authority and Abbie knew that she wasn't the only one to be impressed. His skill in his own field could be in little doubt and she felt a sudden surge of pride which surprised her.

Nick had nothing to do with her any more, she told herself sternly, yet she couldn't help but think back to the days when he'd confided his dreams to her...

'Penny for them?'

She started as she realised that Nick was speaking to her. Sam had got up to go and buy them all another drink and James had gone with him to help carry the glasses. Abbie felt the heat rush to her face as she saw the curiosity in Nick's eyes as he watched her.

'Oh, they're not worth a penny. I was miles away,' she hedged.

'Were you?' He smiled wistfully. 'It seems a lifetime since you and I lay under the old oak tree, planning what we were going to do with our lives, doesn't it?'

'How did you know—?' She stopped abruptly and heard him laugh hollowly.

'What you were thinking?' His eyes held hers in a look she couldn't break. 'I always knew what you were thinking, Abbie.'

It would have sounded arrogant coming from anyone else but not from him because it was true. Once she and Nick had been so close that they'd been able to communicate without words.

Could they still do that? She found herself wondering, and felt an immediate chill at the thought.

She quickly changed the subject. 'What made you decide to come tonight?' she asked instead. 'I didn't get the impression earlier on that you felt much like socialising.'

'I didn't. But I thought it might earn me a few brownie points.'

'Brownie points?' She stared at him in confusion and saw him smile. He ran a hand through his hair, his blue eyes holding a touch of wry self-mockery.

'When you found out that I was making an effort. You said that I had to earn your friendship, Abbie—remember?'

She blushed as she heard the teasing note in his deep voice and he laughed again. 'What was the description you used...? Ah, yes, a "self-centred, peevish, thirty-three-year-old child"! You have a fine turn of phrase but, then, you always did say exactly what you thought. It was one of the things I loved most about you.'

Her heart seemed to jump into her throat as she heard what he'd said. Deep down she knew that she should let it pass but suddenly it was too important that she know the truth. 'Did you love me, Nick?'

He met her gaze for a moment then looked down at his glass, and his voice was flat when he answered. 'Yes, I loved you, Abbie. But that was a long time ago now, wasn't it?'

He looked up as the others arrived with the drinks, responding pleasantly to something Sam said. Abbie didn't hear what it was. She couldn't seem to think straight, let alone join in with the conversation.

She hurriedly finished her drink and stood up, fixing a smile to her face so that nobody would guess how she felt inside. 'Right, that's me finished for the night. I'm dead on my feet. I'll see you all whenever.'

She left the pub and quickly walked home. It had stopped raining, although the sky was patched with clouds and the air felt cool and damp against her face. She let herself into the house and went straight upstairs to get ready for bed.

She lay in the darkness while tears slid silently down her face. Nick had been right. It had been a long time ago, but it didn't stop her wishing that things might have turned out differently for them...

CHAPTER THREE

ABBIE didn't see anything more of Nick for over a week, although that didn't stop her thinking about him. Far too often she found her thoughts drifting back to what he'd said at the pub. Many years ago she'd convinced herself that Nick had never really loved her. Now she knew that she'd been wrong and it seemed to turn her world upside down. It might have helped if she could have put him out of her mind but almost daily someone mentioned his name.

The people of Yewdale were understandably interested in how he was getting on and, apparently, believed that she'd have an inside track on any news. Marion Rimmer, the town busybody, was obviously of that opinion. A septic boil which needed daily dressing proved the perfect opportunity for Marion to pump her for information.

'So, is Nick going to be staying here for good now?' Marion asked as she settled herself in a chair while Abbie carefully peeled away the soiled dressing.

'I'm sure I don't know, Mrs Rimmer,' Abbie replied as she examined the boil. 'That's coming along nicely. I'll put a fresh dressing on it, but it should have cleared up in another day or two. Can you just tilt your head over to the side?'

Marion did as she was told but it didn't stop her talking. 'I was speaking to Peg Ryan the other day. Did you know she's been cleaning at the Delaneys' house? She was telling me that Major Delaney has had the swimming pool cleaned out so Nick can use it. I said to her that I couldn't see as it was possible, not with him being crippled, like. I don't suppose there's much he can do other than sit in that there chair—Ouch!'

'Sorry,' Abbie apologised immediately. She took a quick breath, telling herself that it was silly to let Marion's thoughtless comments upset her. 'Just hold still, will you?' She carefully applied the new dressing and taped it in place, then cleared everything away as Marion got up to look in the mirror over the mantelpiece.

'Mmm, that looks all right, I suppose,' the old lady pronounced. 'Anyway, to get back to Nick, do you see any point in spending all that money on getting the pool cleaned out? Not that the Delaneys are short of a pound or two, but it seems such a waste to me.'

'Hydrotherapy can be very useful for many conditions, Mrs Rimmer. There's no reason why Nick can't still swim, and the exercise will be invaluable in keeping his muscles toned up in the event that he regains the use of his legs,' she explained quietly.

'Doesn't seem much likelihood of that. Peg was saying that the doctors have only given him a slim chance of ever walking again. That's probably why his fiancée broke off their engagement,' Marion declared, still poking away at the wad of gauze on her neck.

'Nick was engaged?' The question came out before Abbie could stop it, and she saw Marion's eyes brighten with interest. She busied herself packing everything into her case but her thoughts were whirling. She'd had no idea that Nick had been engaged, and the discovery shocked her more than it should have done. After all, he was a handsome, intelligent man who must have had his fair share of women over the years, she reasoned, only that thought made her feel little better.

'Didn't you know? Now, that does surprise me, you being such a good friend of his as well.' Marion was obviously relishing the fact that she'd been the one to break the news.

'Nick and I haven't seen one another for a long time, Mrs Rimmer, so we haven't had chance to catch up on what's been happening yet.' She fixed a polite smile to her face to hide the confusion she felt. 'I'll call in about the same time tomorrow, if that's all right with you.'

'Yes, that's fine. The sooner this has cleared up, the better.' Marion was obviously disappointed that she wasn't going to get any more out of Abbie. She went to the window and drew back the lace curtain to peer into the street. 'At least it's not raining. Have you got very far to go to your next call?' she asked guilelessly.

'No, not far.' Abbie smiled to herself. She was too old a hand at dealing with Marion to be caught out that way, and had no intention of passing on any information about who was next on her list! 'Right, I'll see you tomorrow, then…'

'Oh, there's that Adrian again.' Marion let the curtain drop and quickly stepped back from the window.

'Adrian Shaw, do you mean?' Abbie went to the window, but when she went to look out to the street Marion stopped her.

'No, don't let him see you watching!' she warned, an expression of alarm crossing her face. 'I just happened to be watching out for the postman the other day and that boy must have thought I was looking at him. He…he gave me such a funny look, he did.'

'Really?' Abbie frowned as she tried to decide if Marion was making it up, but her anxiety seemed genuine.

'Yes. He used to be a nice enough lad but he's changed. Maybe that's what living in London does to you,' she added sagely. 'All that hustle and bustle and nobody who cares what you do. No wonder folk start acting strangely.'

'Maybe.' Abbie agreed because it was simpler than arguing the point. Adrian's parents had put it around town that their son was away in London, studying, rather than letting the real reason for his absence be known. Not that she blamed them because a lot of people would find it hard to accept the boy's illness. However, she was a little concerned as she left Marion Rimmer's house, and made a mental note to mention Adrian's behaviour when she got back to the surgery.

Her next call was at the Shepherds' house, although not to see Frank, who was recovering well from his injuries. His daughter, Trisha, had recently been diagnosed as diabetic and Abbie was calling in twice a day to give her her injections of insulin. Eventually, Trisha would be able to give herself the injections but so far she'd proved to be very nervous about doing that so patience was needed.

Abbie had a word with Frank, then took Trisha into the dining-room and laid out what she needed on the table. 'Right, I just want to check your blood glucose level, Trisha. You need to do that each day before you give yourself a shot of insulin,' she explained once again.

Wordlessly, Trisha held out her hand and closed her eyes. Even the process of having her finger pricked to gather the necessary drop of blood was an ordeal for her and Abbie's heart went out to the girl. Trisha was only seventeen and her illness had come as a shock to her and her family, especially as her twin brother, Danny, had showed no signs of also being diabetic.

'I hate being like this!' Trisha declared hotly as Abbie inserted the chemically coated strip containing the drop of blood into the monitor to obtain a reading. 'It just isn't fair!'

'It isn't, Trisha, but I'm afraid there isn't a thing anyone can do other than deal with your illness. I know it must seem dreadful to you, but once you get used to regulating your carbohydrate intake and taking the correct dose of insulin, being diabetic shouldn't alter your life all that much,' she said soothingly.

'Of course it will!' Tears flooded Trisha's eyes. 'I have to keep having these horrible injections, don't I? Everyone at school is going to know for starters.'

'I don't see why they should if you don't choose to tell them,' Abbie countered as she got out a syringe and drew up the dose of insulin. 'Obviously, your teachers have to be informed but it's up to you whether or not you tell your friends. Once you learn to do your own injections then you can do so in private and nobody need know if you don't want them to.'

'It's the thought of the injections that's worst!' Trisha shuddered. 'I just hate needles and the thought of having to stick a needle into myself every day scares me.'

'There's no need to be scared, love. It's very simple. And it hardly hurts at all, I promise you. Let me give you this injection, then you can practise.' She swiftly swabbed Trisha's arm and administered the injection, then slipped the used syringe into her sharps box. Taking an orange from the fruit dish in the centre of the table, she held it out. 'Right, we'll pretend this orange is your arm, OK?'

Trisha giggled. 'If you say so.'

Abbie smiled, pleased to see that the girl looked a little more cheerful. 'Dr Allen has recommended that you use an insulin pen so we'll practise with that so you can get used to it. It's really easy to use as all you need to do is insert a fresh cartridge each time you give yourself a dose of insulin. But for now we'll use the pen without the cartridge.'

She demonstrated how to slip the needle into the skin of the fruit then let Trisha try it. The girl was obviously nervous at first, but after several attempts was soon managing quite well.

'Good! You're really getting the hang of it now. And

that's how easy it'll be when you have to do it to yourself,' she assured her.

'It wasn't as hard as I thought it would be,' Trisha admitted. 'Although it's bound to be different when it's my arm I'm sticking that needle into!'

'Of course it will. But if you know how to do it properly then it won't hurt any more than if you pricked yourself when sewing. Anyway, you keep on practising. By the end of the week I'll bet you a pound that you're ready to go solo!'

Trisha laughed. 'I don't know if I want to win or lose that bet, but I'll keep practising. I want to go back to school before I miss too much work.'

'You're doing A levels, aren't you?' Abbie asked as she cleared up.

'Yes, next summer. I'm hoping to go to university so I daren't get behind. We'll be sending in our applications for places soon as well,' Trisha explained.

'Then get practising with that fruit! Once you get the hang of it you'll wonder why you were scared, believe me.' Abbie gave her a last encouraging smile then went to say goodbye to Frank and left. She checked her watch and was surprised to see that it was almost lunchtime. She had a half-day that day and there was just one last visit to do, checking the ulcer on Jack Marsh's leg once again, and then she was finished.

She did the call, pleased to find that her careful treatment had paid off and that Jack wouldn't need another visit. She got into her car and headed home, wondering what to do with her free afternoon.

There was always housework to catch up with, not to mention a pile of ironing which was growing as the days passed, but she was reluctant to stay indoors and waste the day. A strong wind had blown away the rainclouds and the sky had a washed-clean freshness that was too tempting to resist.

She made herself a sandwich when she got in then changed into jeans and a thick creamy wool sweater she'd had for years. Her old wax jacket was on the peg behind the door, her equally old walking boots outside in the porch. Within twenty minutes of arriving home she was out of the house again but this time she left her car behind. A good stiff walk was the order of the day and would help her unwind.

An hour later Abbie stopped on the banks of Yewdale Water. Although it was mid-week there were several cars drawn up along the bank and she could see people wading into the water with oxygen cylinders strapped to their backs. The lake was often used for underwater diving as it was very deep near the centre. She watched the divers disappear two at a time beneath the grey-green water and shivered. It was a sport which had never appealed to her.

Another car drew up and she glanced casually towards it unable to hide her surprise as she recognised the driver. Nick seemed equally surprised to see her because he rolled down his window immediately.

'What are you doing here?' he demanded in a tone which didn't make her think that he was pleased to see her.

'I could ask you the same thing,' she replied lightly to disguise the pang she felt. So much for him wanting them to be friends! She went over to the car, however, unable to hide her curiosity. 'I didn't know you were driving again, Nick.'

'It's my first time out apart from a few lessons to get used to the modifications.' He opened the door so that she could see how everything had been adapted for his use. 'All the controls are operated by hand and it's an automatic gear change as well.'

'It must feel odd at first,' Abbie mused. 'I can't imagine

not using my feet—' She stopped abruptly as she realised how tactless that had been. 'I'm sorry, Nick—'

'Forget it.' He cut short her apology, his face giving little away as he looked towards the lake. 'What are you doing here anyway? I'd have thought you'd be working.'

'I had time owing to me so I've taken a half-day off,' she explained flatly, hurt by his abruptness. 'It was either doing the housework or going out so you can see which won.'

He laughed softly. 'No contest, in my opinion. One thing I used to hate was catching up on all the chores around the flat. There were so many other things I'd rather have been doing than washing and ironing and all the other hundred and one boring jobs.'

'You didn't have anyone to share the work with you, then?' she asked without thinking, then felt her face heat as he turned to give her a frowning look.

'What do you mean?' he asked tersely.

'Oh, just that I'd have thought you'd have a…a house-keeper or something,' she stammered, wishing she'd held her tongue rather than bring up the subject of his fiancée so clumsily.

'You always were a bad liar, Abbie. I expect you've heard that I was engaged and that my fiancée broke off the engagement after the accident?'

'I'm sure it isn't any of my business…' she began stiffly.

'It isn't anyone's business except mine but that won't stop people talking, will it?' His face tautened as he stared towards the lake again. 'Maybe I should tell you the true version so that you can spread it around. That way it will save a lot of lurid speculation.'

'I've just told you that it hasn't anything to do with me. And for your information I only heard about it this morning. I didn't even know you were engaged before that,' she retorted, hating the way he was making her feel in the wrong. She swung round, her pretty face set as she zipped up her jacket. 'Anyway, it's time I was off…'

'No, don't go. I'm sorry, Abbie. I didn't mean to bite your head off. You're the last person in this town who'd go spreading gossip.'

There was no denying the contrition in his voice and she paused. She turned to look at him and saw the wry smile that touched his mobile mouth. For a moment he looked so like the Nick she'd known that her heart turned over. It must have hurt him unbearably if his fiancée had walked out on him because of the accident, she thought sadly. Although she couldn't imagine any woman doing that to the man she loved.

She gave him a tentative smile, 'Want to talk about it? It might help and not because it will put the facts straight for the gossip-mongers. Whatever you tell me, Nick, is strictly between you and me.'

'I know that.' He sighed heavily. 'Look, I hate to ask, but do you think you could help me? As I say, this is my first time out in the car and I'm not used to the logistics of getting myself into the damned chair so I'm rather stuck here. It would be good to get out and sit by the water for a while,' he added wistfully.

'Of course I'll help. You don't need to ask,' she replied immediately. Following his instructions, she lifted the collapsible wheelchair from behind his seat. It was quite easy to do as the footwell had been filled in so that the light-weight chair didn't need to be lifted over the door sill. With a bit of practice Nick would be able to do it himself without much difficulty but for now she was glad to help.

She put it next to the driver's side while he levered himself into it. It was all done in a matter of minutes and he grinned in relief as he lowered the armrest into place. 'Even easier than I'd thought it would be. Thanks, Abbie.'

'Do you want a push? It's a bit rough getting over that

shingle,' she offered, wondering if she was doing the right thing. Nick was obviously sensitive about asking for help but, surprisingly, he accepted with alacrity.

She pushed the chair towards the lake. It was hard going over the loose shingle even though he did his best to help by manually turning the chair's wheels. He grinned as he heard her puffing as they finally reached the water's edge.

'Not bad for a beginner,' he teased, 'although you could do with building up a bit of muscle…'

'Cheeky monkey! If you didn't weigh ten tons it would be a whole lot easier.' She ducked as he aimed a clip at her ear and was still laughing as she sat down beside him on the shingle. It was odd that they could laugh about this, she thought in amazement. What had happened was so tragic and yet he was still Nick, still the same man he'd always been. It made it all the more difficult to understand why his fiancée had acted the way she had. Suddenly, she knew that she had to find out why.

'So, what happened, Nick?' she asked softly, watching his face.

'With Jill and me?' His tone was flat after the laughter of a few moments earlier. It was obvious that the memory still hurt and Abbie felt a pain she didn't try to understand shoot through her heart. On a subconscious level she knew that it wasn't just because she was sorry for the way he'd been hurt so badly but she didn't dare examine her feelings too closely.

He gave a heavy sigh as he ran a hand through his hair to brush it back from his forehead. He was wearing cords and a thick navy blue sweater with a paler blue shirt beneath it. The colour suited him, bringing out the sapphire blue in his dark eyes and enhancing his faint tan. He looked so handsome and so…so vital that Abbie found it hard to accept that he couldn't walk. It was only the chair that was a sharp reminder of how his life had changed so drastically in the past months.

'Jill decided that she couldn't tie herself to an invalid. She was quite open and honest about her decision and I respect her for that,' he stated flatly. 'I also understood her reasons. She's in advertising, and her job entails long hours and a lot of travelling. The last thing she needs is to come home to someone who needs taking care of.'

'But surely you could have found a way round that?' Abbie argued. 'You could have hired someone to help you if she found that aspect difficult to deal with.'

'It wasn't just that, nor was it only Jill who thought it better we ended our relationship.'

'What do you mean? Are you saying that you wanted your engagement to be called off, Nick?' she queried in surprise.

'Yes. It seemed the best thing to do.' He turned to look at her and there was a total absence of emotion in his eyes which told her how difficult he was finding this. 'I have no idea if I can ever be a proper husband to any woman, Abbie. It wouldn't have been fair to Jill to expect her to live in a platonic relationship.'

'I...I see.' Her voice was little more than a whisper as his words sank in. She felt overwhelmed with sadness for him. 'What have the doctors said about...about...?'

'Whether or not I'll ever be able to make love to a woman again?' He laughed bitterly. 'Not a lot. It's really a question of waiting and seeing once again. However, that didn't seem the best prognosis for a happy marriage so we both decided to call the wedding off.'

'But surely if they said that then there's still a hope that things will work out?' Abbie disputed.

'Like the one I was given that I'll walk again? Few women would happily accept those odds, Abbie!' he mocked.

She would have done! No matter how slight the chance, she would never have turned her back on the man she loved. It was on the tip of her tongue to say so but something stopped her. What good would it do Nick to hear that? They were the words he needed to hear from the woman he loved, not from her. The realisation hurt unbearably.

'Anyway, enough about me and my problems. Tell me about your marriage, Abbie. What went wrong?'

She shrugged, avoiding his eyes as she stared across the lake in case he saw some glimmer of what she'd been thinking. 'It just didn't work out, that's all.'

'Yet you made sure all the right ingredients were there, didn't you?'

She frowned as she turned to look at him. 'What do you mean by that?'

'Exactly what I said. You were never someone who made a spur-of-the-moment decision, Abbie. You took care to weigh things up, work them out, cover all angles—as I know only too well.'

Her face heated as she suddenly understood what he was alluding to, and he laughed softly. 'Yes. Remember when I asked you to live with me? You were just eighteen and I was in my first year in med school and missing you like crazy. I came home for your birthday and asked you if you'd come back to London with me and you refused. You said that it was silly for us to rush into things, that there was no hope of a relationship lasting when we had nothing to fall back on. We had no money, no place to live—nothing at all to guarantee that we could make a success of it.

'I think what hit me hardest was that you overlooked the one thing we had going for us.'

She didn't ask what he meant because there was no need. She'd loved Nick and in those days she'd believed he'd loved her, enough to understand her fears if nothing else.

She'd seen other relationships flounder through lack of money and the subsequent arguments, her own parents' marriage being one of them.

She'd been only a small child when her father had walked out but it had left a lasting impression on her. It was little wonder she'd been afraid that she and Nick could finish up the same way. Yet in the end it had been her fear which had ruined everything because Nick had taken her refusal badly.

He'd stopped coming home, then eventually had stopped writing. Abbie had felt as though her world had fallen apart. Only by devoting herself to her nurse's training had she got through that painful period. She'd met Paul at the hospital when he'd been a patient and had liked his easy charm and confident manner. He'd held down a good job as well, and had offered her the security she'd thought so important. Their marriage had had all the right ingredients except the most important one of all—she'd never really loved Paul.

'Still, that's all water under the bridge now, isn't it? We were just kids then and I suppose you were right.' His easy dismissal simply added to her pain but she tried not to let it show.

'Probably,' she concurred.

'At least it means that we can still behave in a civilised fashion around one another,' he continued, piling on the agony, albeit unknowingly. He looked up in evident surprise as she got to her feet so she told herself that she'd imagined the pensive note in his voice. 'Something wrong, Abbie?'

'No, of course not!' she said with a laugh that sounded like something out of a badly acted play, too high-pitched to be convincing. She rushed on. 'I thought I'd try my hand at a game of ducks and drakes. Fancy a go?'

'Is that a challenge?' He grinned at her. 'I suppose you reckon that I'm a pushover by being somewhat handicapped by this chair. If so then you're in for a surprise, Nurse Fraser!'

'Oh, yes? All talk and no action, I'll bet!' She picked up a handful of pebbles, glad that the subject had been dropped. She found talking about the past, both hers and Nick's, rather too painful. 'Would you like me to go first just so you can see how it's done?'

'Be my guest. But you could regret giving me the advantage,' he shot back, leaning over to pick up an even larger handful of stones. 'While you're practising your shots I'll just be sorting through this little lot to find some decent stones…'

Abbie laughed as she turned towards the water, her previous sadness lifting a little. She'd forgotten what good fun Nick could be and how he'd always had this ability to cheer her up. Testing a pebble in her hand, she tossed it towards the water then groaned as it immediately sank without even the smallest bounce. A second pebble and then a third didn't achieve any better results either.

'Tut-tut, what a dismal show. But, then, you never were much good at this. I think you need a little tuition and then maybe you'll manage to get at least one bounce off the water,' he crowed.

He rolled the chair closer to the water's edge and angled it so that he could toss her pebble into the lake. It bounced just once, before disappearing, and Abbie sighed.

'I don't know about giving *me* tuition. This is hardly what you'd call a master class in the age-old art, is it?' she taunted.

'I was just getting a feel for the water. This is a very exact science—a lot of people don't appreciate that,' he retorted.

'Science? Come on, any six-year-old kid could have done better!' She swung round with a heavy sigh and made to walk away. 'Doesn't seem much point in wasting my time here…'

'Don't you believe it!' His hand snaked out and closed around hers with a speed that brought her up short. Abbie felt the thrill of awareness rocket from her fingers to every cell in her body. Her breath seemed to be caught deep inside her, making her lungs burn with the unaccustomed pressure.

Then Nick let her go, bending down to pick up another handful of pebbles so that she couldn't see his expression, yet she heard the grating note in his voice which told her that he wasn't immune to what had just happened either.

'Stand right there and watch the master at work. You're going to have to eat your words, Abbie Fraser…'

The pebble skimmed the water, sending up puffs of spray as it bounced over a dozen times, before finally sinking. Abbie watched it disappear from sight but for a moment didn't say anything. She wanted to be sure that her voice gave nothing away when she did speak, but how could she be sure of anything any more when she didn't understand what was happening to her…?

'Don't, Abbie. There's no point. It's far too late to go back. It would be a mistake to try, especially now.'

They had always been honest with one another and it seemed that nothing had changed in that respect. She wished that it had but Nick's honesty demanded hers in return. 'I just never expected this,' she admitted softly.

'That we should feel the odd frisson when we touch?' His tone was warm and smoky, his face holding a tenderness which made her ache because it was so familiar. How many times had he looked at her with that same expression on his face? She had no idea but she realised suddenly how much she'd missed it.

'You and I loved each other once, Abbie. It's only natural that there's the odd spark left. Each and every relationship we have in our lives leaves its mark.' His tone was cool now and she shivered as she heard it.

'That sounds like a professional opinion rather than a personal one.'

'Probably a bit of both. Understanding *why* we think the way we do doesn't make anyone immune, not even a psychiatrist. In fact, to be good at the job you have to be able to empathise with what your patients are feeling.' He turned to look at the lake. 'It would be very easy for both of us to try to pick up where we left off, but neither of us could be sure we were doing it for the right reason. I would never play upon your sympathy, Abbie.'

Her eyes misted as she heard the pain in his voice. 'Maybe it isn't only sympathy I feel, Nick.'

'I doubt that.' His tone was flat. 'Anyone who's confronted with this kind of situation feels all sorts of things, ranging from guilt because he or she isn't the one injured to a desire to make amends in some way. It isn't the best yardstick to measure one's feelings by, believe me.'

She wanted to deny what he'd said but she knew it could hold a grain of truth. Seeing Nick injured like this, it had awoken all her natural sympathy and it would be easy to confuse that with something else. She couldn't still love him after all this time! It was ridiculous even to think that. And yet the way she'd responded instantly to his touch was hard to understand when she'd never responded that way to Paul.

'Well, now that I've proved my superiority I suppose I'd better start heading back home.' He grinned as he saw the startled look she shot him. 'I meant at ducks and drakes, Abbie.'

She laughed as he'd intended her to do. 'Thank heavens for that! I thought you were getting delusions of grandeur, although I'm not sure if that's an expression an eminent psychiatrist would approve of.'

He rolled his eyes at the less than subtle gibe. 'Neither am I. Good job it's only me you're talking to, isn't it? Some of my learned colleagues would have your guts for garters for making such a snap diagnosis—'

He broke off all of a sudden, his eyes narrowing as he stared towards the lake. 'What's going on there? Looks like there's some sort of a problem.'

Abbie turned to follow his gaze and frowned as she saw the knot of divers that had surfaced from the water. They seemed very agitated, one in particular struggling and thrashing about despite the others' attempts to hold him. 'Something does seem to be wrong, doesn't it? I wonder what's happened.'

They watched in concern as the party waded back to shore. The diver who'd been struggling collapsed as they reached the beach and had to be carried clear of the water by his friends.

'What happened?' Nick demanded, moving his chair closer to the group.

'He surfaced too fast. I tried to warn him but he panicked,' one of them replied, ripping off his face mask. 'Dave, can you hear me? Where does it hurt, man?'

'My chest…' The stricken diver groaned as he clutched his chest. Abbie hurried over to the group and dropped on her knees beside them.

'I'm a nurse and that gentleman over there is a doctor. Let me take a look at your friend,' she ordered. She quickly checked the man's pulse then looked at Nick. 'Very rapid and thready, and he's obviously having problems breathing.'

'How deep were you?' he demanded, looking at the other divers.

'Fifteen…twenty metres. It's deeper in the centre of that lake than we realised,' the spokesman answered, sounding worried. 'How are you now, mate?' he asked, turning to his friend.

'I can't see properly and it feels as though my chest is being crushed…' the man replied on a moan.

Nick's face was grim as he looked at her. 'He's suffering from decompression sickness through surfacing too fast, by the look of it. Nitrogen from the compressed air he was breathing has formed bubbles in his body tissue and must be blocking the blood vessels. We need to get him to a recompression chamber as fast as possible otherwise he'll die.'

'I'll alert the emergency services. I've no idea where the nearest recompression chamber is, though,' she added worriedly, getting to her feet.

'There's one in Merseyside. The coastguard will know that. Just tell them we've got a diver who's surfaced from approximately twenty metres so that they can get everything ready,' he instructed, taking charge with an easy authority that spoke volumes. He turned to the men. 'Have any of you got a mobile phone with you? No? Then one of you will have to drive Nurse Fraser to get help.'

'I'll do it,' the spokesman offered immediately. Shrugging off his air tanks, he set off at a run towards the cars. Abbie went to follow him then stopped when Nick caught hold of her hand.

'Take care, Abbie. Don't let him drive too fast. We don't want any more accidents.'

She knew he didn't mean just the accident in the water and she paused to reassure him. 'Don't worry, Nick. I'll be fine.'

'Good.' He let her go and turned his attention back to the man lying on the shingle, quickly instructing the man's friends to get something to cover him up with to keep him warm.

Abbie shot a last look at his bent head then turned and

ran to the car, trying to rationalise the warm glow which was spreading through her whole body. Naturally Nick would worry about anyone's safety and yet there had been just that little extra concern in his eyes which he hadn't been able to hide...

CHAPTER FOUR

QUITE a crowd had gathered at the lake by the time the convoy of ambulance and police outriders set off. Abbie had gone to the Outward Bound centre to make the emergency call as it had been the nearest place she could think of.

Ian Farnsworth, the centre manager, drove her back to the lake when the trauma suddenly caught up with the diver's friend. He stayed behind while Ian's wife, Barbara, plied him with hot tea and lent a sympathetic ear.

There was a party of sport science students staying at the centre that week and most of them followed on to watch the drama unfolding. The stricken diver was being transported by road to the recompression chamber on the Wirral as it was deemed too risky to fly him there by helicopter, although it would have been faster. Any further changes in the air pressure could have disastrous consequences for the man.

'Well, fingers crossed that he makes it,' Ian observed as the convoy drove away with blue lights flashing at front and rear. 'How long will it take them to get there, do you think?'

'Two, possibly two and half hours, depending on the traffic,' Nick replied. 'The police officer in charge said that they'd put traffic control on full alert and they'd clear the route for them. Most of it's by motorway so they should make good time.'

'But will he last that long?' Abbie asked worriedly. 'He was in such pain...'

'He should make it,' Nick assured her. 'He has the advantage of being fairly close to the facilities he needs so we'll just have to keep our fingers crossed, as Ian said.'

Most of the onlookers were drifting away now and the rest of the divers were stowing their gear into their cars. They came over to thank Abbie and Nick for their help, then Ian offered to show them the way to the centre so they could collect their friend. Evidently, the plan was that they'd drive to Merseyside to find out what was happening to Dave, the injured diver.

It was a bit of an anticlimax when the area around the lake was quiet once more. Abbie sighed as she looked at the peaceful scene. 'It seems hard to believe that something like that can happen out of the blue, doesn't it?'

'It does, indeed. But, then, nobody can predict an accident.' Nick's tone was flat and she realised that he was thinking about what had happened to him, but there wasn't anything she could say to make the memory easier to bear. They didn't say anything else as they made their way back to his car.

It was a little more difficult getting Nick back into the driving seat than it had been getting him out. Abbie frowned as she saw how grey he looked and how deeply etched the lines around his mouth were. 'Are you OK?'

'Yes,' he began immediately then sighed. 'No, if you want the truth. I feel like hell. I've been leading such a quiet life lately that I can't keep up with all this excitement,' he joked, trying to make light of it.

'You should have said, Nick!' She quickly stowed the chair in the back of the car, before walking round to the passenger side. She got in and gave him a stern look. 'You mustn't go pushing yourself too hard too soon.'

'Yes, Nurse!' He grinned to take the sting out of the words but it didn't disguise the tiredness on his face. 'Are you always this bossy?'

'Always!' she replied tartly. 'Ask anyone and they'll tell

you the same thing—that Abbie Fraser excels at telling people what to do and when to do it. And right now I'm telling you that you need to get home and rest. All right?'

'It will have to be, won't it?' he replied wryly as he started the engine. 'I don't think I feel up to arguing at this moment. You certainly know how to catch a guy at a low point…'

Abbie smiled as she settled back in the seat. It was good to see that he could laugh about his predicament although that didn't mean he'd accepted it yet. He was just trying to make an effort for her sake and her heart warmed at the thought.

They kept up an easy, non-demanding conversation as they drove back to Yewdale. It was already growing dusk and he had to switch on his headlights as they reached the outskirts of the town. Abbie got ready to jump out when they reached his house but he didn't stop.

'Where are we going?' she demanded in surprise as he drove past the gates.

'I'm taking you home, of course.' He paused at the crossroads, waiting for a gap in the traffic before turning right and heading towards her home.

'Don't be silly, Nick. I'm perfectly able to make my own way home—' she began.

'I'm sure you are. However, I'm not so damned tired that I'll let you walk when I can give you a lift.' His mouth set into a grim line which warned her not to pursue the matter so she held her tongue. Obviously, Nick saw it as his masculine duty to see her home safely, even though he was completely worn out!

He drew up in front of the house and his eyes were very dark as they skimmed over her set face. 'You know, the worst thing of all about this accident, Abbie, is the fact that people keep trying to make decisions for me. I know they mean well but it doesn't help how I feel about myself. God knows, it's bad enough knowing that you're only half a man without being treated like one.'

'I never meant to do that, Nick—' she demurred, but he cut her off.

'No, you didn't. But just answer me one question— would you have given it a second thought if I'd driven you home before I had the accident?' He laughed harshly when she didn't answer. 'See what I mean? It affects the way everyone sees me and that's what I hate most of all.'

'I know it must be hard for you. But you're wrong, Nick. I don't see you any differently.'

'Oh, spare me the platitudes!' He leaned over to open the door for her. 'Forgive me for not getting out. This is the best I can do, I'm afraid.'

She sucked in a great breath of air, incensed by his refusal to believe her. 'You really are the most pig-headed man I know! I don't know why I'm even bothering trying to convince you.'

'Neither do I,' he shot back, turning to glare at her at the very moment that she moved to get out. They were suddenly so close that she could see tiny images of herself reflected in his eyes and smell the faint tang of soap which clung to his skin. Her mind seemed to whirl, flashes from the past merging with the present as she recalled other times when they'd been this close...what had happened next...

He drew back abruptly and his voice was as hard as steel. 'I have no illusions, Abbie. Now, I think it's time I got home. It's been a tiring day.'

She got out of the car without a word and let herself into the house, not watching him drive away. Nick wouldn't want her to do that, as he didn't want her reassurances that his disability hadn't changed how she viewed him. After all, she wasn't the woman he loved and that was what mattered...

* * *

'Sounds like you and Nick had fun yesterday.'

Abbie was checking her list of calls when Sam came into the surgery the following morning. She'd spent a sleepless night going over and over everything that had happened the day before, wishing that she'd handled things better.

She was expecting too much to hope that Nick had got over the accident so soon. It would take him months to come to terms with it and he was bound to feel different about himself and his role in society. And yet she hated to think that he believed anyone would find him less of a man than he had been before—

'Abbie?'

She jumped as Sam suddenly reminded her that she hadn't answered his question. She gave a dismissive shrug. 'It was a bit hairy, I have to admit. The worst thing was not being able to do anything for that poor diver.'

'From what I heard, you two did everything possible. You got him the help he needed and did so quickly,' Sam replied with a frown. 'Is something wrong, Abbie? You look a bit uptight this morning.'

'Of course not! I was just…thinking about the amount of work I have to do today, that's all,' she quickly ad libbed.

'Sure?' He leaned against the desk and folded his arms as he continued to study her.

'What is this? The Spanish Inquisition?' she demanded with a trace of acerbity. She and Sam were good friends but she didn't want to discuss her feelings with him or anyone.

'I'm just worried about you, that's all,' he replied, without taking offence at her attempts to brush aside his questions.

She sighed heavily. 'Thanks, Sam. I don't mean to snap but this is something I have to work out myself, you understand.'

'It's got something to do with Nick Delaney, hasn't it?'
He laughed when he saw her colour rise. 'You've been
acting oddly ever since you heard about his accident so that
isn't an example of my remarkable intuition.'

She smiled as he'd intended her to. 'More of a lucky
guess, I'd say.'

'So, I am right, then? What's the matter? Did you and
Delaney have something going for you at one time? Is that
what the problem is?'

'Not really,' she answered evasively. 'Nick and I grew
up together. We were friends for years. I just wish I could
convince him that life still has so much to offer him, but
it isn't easy.'

'The accident is bound to have had a devastating effect
on him. It's unrealistic to expect him to have adapted to
the situation just yet.'

'I suppose you're right. But he seems to think that people
see him as less of a person just because he can't walk. He
even told me that he feels half a man now!' she added
hotly.

'Obviously, you don't agree.' Sam was watching her
closely—too closely, in fact. She turned away with a shrug,
scooping up the rest of the papers she'd been sorting
through and dropping them into the tray for filing.

'You know the answer, Abbie? You have to convince
Nick that in your eyes nothing has changed and that you
still see him as the person he's always been.'

'I don't think it's my opinion that matters,' she stated
flatly.

'What do you mean by that? Of course it matters…' Sam
stopped as the door opened and David appeared.

'Morning, you two. Everything all right?' he asked,
shrugging off his jacket.

'Fine. How's Laura?' she asked quickly, glad of the excuse to put an end to the conversation. Sam meant well and

he'd never repeat a word she told him, but it didn't feel right to break Nick's confidence by discussing his broken engagement.

'Blooming is the word!' David laughed. 'Not a trace of morning sickness so far. In fact, if it weren't for the bump I wouldn't believe she was pregnant. Oh, that reminds me, Laura said to tell you that you're all invited to a house-warming supper on Saturday. We're just about straight at long last, and ready for visitors.'

'It must be odd, moving into the house next door,' Abbie mused. David had met Laura when she'd bought the house next door to his. He'd been a widower at the time and after they'd married they'd decided to sell his house and move into hers.

'It is and it isn't, if that makes sense. Obviously, my old house held a lot of memories, but both of us are looking forward to making a fresh start,' he explained. 'And Mike and Emily are thrilled by the move, funnily enough,' he added, referring to the two of this three children who were still living at home. 'They seem to think it's a great adventure.'

'And Holly thinks it's a great idea, too,' Sam added. He'd recently become engaged to David's eldest daughter, Holly, and the warmth of his tone was a good indication of his feelings for her. 'I spoke to her last night on the phone and she's really pleased about it.'

'I know.' David clapped Sam on the shoulder. 'Mind you, that daughter of mine has her head so far in the clouds at the moment, thanks to you, that I don't think she'd have worried if I'd told her we were moving to Outer Mongolia! The joys of young love, eh?'

'Listen who's talking?' Abbie teased. 'You and Laura are like a couple of starry-eyed teenagers.' She looked round as the door opened again and groaned as Elizabeth and James came in, holding hands. 'In fact, I'm the only one round here who hasn't been bitten by the love bug. Thank heavens one of us still has her feet firmly planted on the ground.'

'Don't sound so smug,' Sam shot back. 'Nobody is immune to this disease. It strikes when you least expect it to.'

She rolled her eyes to signal that she didn't believe a word of it. However, her smile soon faded as she left the surgery. Over the past few months she'd seen her best friends fall in love and she wouldn't have been human if she hadn't felt a bit left out at times. Having someone to share things with, that was something she missed, although she and Paul hadn't had that sort of relationship.

There had always been a certain distance between them, a reluctance to confide their innermost thoughts. They'd never been as close as she and Nick had been. The realisation made her feel even sadder.

'That's absolutely brilliant! Well done.' Abbie couldn't hide her delight. Trisha Shepherd had just given herself her very first injection of insulin and she was thrilled that the girl had managed to overcome her fears.

'I practised all yesterday, didn't I, Mum?' Trisha explained.

'She did, indeed. And I've a bowl full of punctured fruit to prove it!' Jeannie Shepherd smiled as she hugged her daughter. 'You're a real star, that's what you are, love. I think we need to celebrate, don't you? How about a trip to Manchester to do some shopping? You're going to need some new clothes for your university interviews.'

'Really? Wow, Mum, thanks!' Trisha gave her mother a bear hug. 'When can we go?'

'Oh, you go and sort that out with your dad.' Jeannie waited until the girl had dashed from the room, before turning to Abbie again. 'I want to thank you for all your patience. Trisha's always been terrified of injections so that this has been the worst thing possible to happen to her. It was such a shock, too.'

'It must have been,' Abbie sympathised. 'However, diabetes is something that can be controlled. So long as Trisha sticks strictly to her diet and the correct dosage of insulin then she shouldn't have any problems.'

'So Dr Allen explained.' Jeannie squared her shoulders. 'Well, it's just something we'll have to get on with so there's no point moithering ourselves about it. Now, how about a cup of tea before you go? Have you got time?'

'Well…' Abbie glanced at her watch and grinned. 'Why not?'

She followed Jeannie to the kitchen and sat down at the table while the older woman made a pot of tea and arranged some chocolate digestives on a plate.

'Oh, I can feel the inches piling on my waistline already,' she groaned as she bit into a biscuit with relish.

'It's my hips where they settle,' Jeannie said with a laugh as she poured the tea. 'I don't care what anyone says— calories *know* how to lodge in all the places you don't want them to— Oh!'

The teapot landed with such a thud on the worktop that Abbie jumped. 'Are you all right, Jeannie? What happened?'

Jeannie pressed a hand to her heart. 'It was that boy again, looking in the window this time. He scared the life out of me.'

'Boy?' She got up to look but there was nobody in the garden.

'That Adrian Shaw, I mean. He keeps hanging around outside the house. I thought I was imagining things at first and then Trisha mentioned that she kept seeing him.'

'Have you spoken to him?' Abbie asked in concern.

Jeannie shook her head. 'No, he walks off if you try to say anything to him. I don't want to cause trouble but I'll have to get Frank to have a word with his parents if it carries on. It's not natural, is it? I mean, why won't he speak to me?'

Abbie shook her head because there was little she could say. It would be unethical to mention Adrian's medical history, although she knew that Jeannie would be sympathetic. Still, it was very worrying all the same.

They chatted about all sorts of things as they drank their tea but when she left she was still thinking about what had happened. She took a good look up and down the road but there was no sign of Adrian. However, when she turned the corner she spotted him huddled in a doorway. She stopped the car and went over to have a word with him, putting out a restraining hand when he went to hurry away.

'No, wait a moment, Adrian. It's all right, I just wanted to say hello and ask how you are. You remember me, don't you—Abbie Fraser, the district nurse?'

'Did they send you?' he demanded, staring at her with open hostility. He was a good head taller than she was and heavily built. His clothes were clean and well cared-for and there was little about his appearance to alarm her but she still felt uneasy. It was something about the expression in his eyes, she realised. A certain detachment which was strangely chilling.

'Nobody sent me, Adrian. I was just driving past and stopped to say hello.'

'They always say that. But I'm not stupid.' He pushed past her and hurried away, quickly disappearing round the corner.

Abbie got back into her car, wondering what she should do. There had been something decidedly odd about Adrian's behaviour, although maybe that was because she knew his history. Was she allowing her knowledge of his schizophrenia to influence her thinking?

She still hadn't decided by the time she got back to the

surgery that night. There were quite a few patients in the waiting-room and she debated whether or not she should stay to have a word with James about Adrian Shaw. In the end she decided that she had to say something because she'd never forgive herself if there was something wrong.

She managed to slip in to see him between appointments and got straight to the point, outlining what had happened at the Shepherds' house and adding what Marion Rimmer had told her as well. 'I just thought I should mention it. I might be worrying unnecessarily, of course.'

'And, there again, you might not.' James sat back in his chair with a sigh. 'You were right to tell me, Abbie. I think I'd better check with his parents that he is taking his medication properly.'

'You think he might have stopped taking it?' she queried.

'It's possible. I've seen it happen before. A patient feels so much better that he doesn't see the need to take his medication any longer so starts to relapse. It's a vicious circle and hard to break. That's why a lot of people are given depot injections of long-acting neuroleptics, but the side effects can be very distressing. Maybe I should have a word with Nick as well. He's the expert after all,' he added pensively.

'Sounds like a good idea. Anyway, I won't keep you any longer.' She headed towards the door, trying to ignore the small frisson which had run through her on hearing Nick's name.

'I'll mention it to Nick on Saturday when I see him. Then you can tell him what you told me.'

She stopped to glance back. 'Saturday?'

'Mmm, David and Laura's housewarming do. Nick's been invited. Turns out that Laura knows him—he's a friend of one of her brothers'.' James laughed. 'It's a small world, isn't it?'

'It is,' she agreed, struggling to keep her tone neutral.

Knowing that Nick would be at the dinner on Saturday, that cast a whole different light on what had been just a pleasant night with friends. She left the surgery, trying to quell the rush of anticipation she felt, but it wouldn't go away.

She'd be seeing Nick again on Saturday and, foolish or not, her heart was already beating faster at the thought!

CHAPTER FIVE

'ABBIE! How lovely to see you. Come in.'

Laura opened the door wide, smiling as Abbie handed her a bottle of wine. 'Oh, you shouldn't have. But thanks anyway.'

'You're looking marvellous, Laura.' Abbie shrugged off her coat and gave that to her as well. 'There's no need to ask if being pregnant agrees with you!'

'I almost feel guilty about how well I've been.' Laura hung the jacket on the hallstand then linked her arm through Abbie's and led her to the sitting-room. 'No more morning sickness at all, touch wood—' She broke off as David appeared. 'Oh, there you are. Sort Abbie out with a drink, will you, darling? I'll just go and prod the roast to see if it's done yet.'

'Of course. Come on in.' David led the way into the sitting-room. 'You're the first one here so what will it be? You may as well get your order in before the others arrive.'

'Sherry, please, if you have it.' She sank onto a huge, squashy sofa and looked round with pleasure. 'This is beautiful, David. I just love the colour of the walls and that fireplace...everything!'

'All Laura's doing.' He grinned wickedly as Laura came into the room, pretending that he hadn't seen her. 'Why do you think I married her? She can turn her hand to anything from decorating to car maintenance. That marriage licence was worth every penny as I'm going to save a fortune, having her around!'

'Don't count your chickens, Scrooge! Wait until all my plans are hatched, before patting yourself on the back. I'm not sure how much it's going to cost to add a conservatory to the back of the house, but I'm sure we'll save a packet if you dig out the foundations!' Laura retorted, winking at Abbie.

'Oh, that's got me right where it hurts—in my wallet *and* my back! Have you no heart, woman?' David protested.

'No, so don't try playing on my sympathy!' Laura laughingly retorted. She kissed him quickly just as the bell rang again. 'Sounds like another of our guests has arrived.'

'I'll get it,' David said quickly. 'I don't want you running around all night, exhausting yourself. Sit down.'

'Yes, sir.' Laura sank onto the sofa as he hurried from the room. 'David would wrap me up in cotton wool if I let him.'

'It's only natural that he should worry about you. He's so thrilled about this baby, isn't he?' Abbie said, although her mind was only half on the conversation. The rest of her was trying to hear what was going on in the hall. Had Nick arrived? she wondered, her heart racing.

'We both are. To think that this time last year we hadn't even met!' Laura looked up as David came back into the room with Elizabeth and James in tow. 'Hello, you two. Welcome to the new Mackenzie Ross residence.'

'This room is just gorgeous!' Elizabeth declared, looking around her with appreciation. 'You're going to have to give me a few tips on interior design, Laura.'

'Are you and James thinking of buying a place of your own, then?' Abbie enquired.

Elizabeth shrugged as she accepted a glass of gin and tonic from David. 'Thanks. We're not sure yet. We've decided to wait until Father is home before we make up our minds. I love the house but the disadvantage of living there is that you're never away from the job, with the surgery being built onto the side of it.'

'I can see how that might be a bit of a problem—' Abbie began, then jumped as the bell rang again. She carefully set her sherry glass down on a side table to avoid spilling it as David excused himself once more and went to answer it.

Elizabeth and James kept up an easy conversation with Laura about the pros and cons of them buying a house while he was gone, but Abbie felt unable to join in. Her every sense was attuned to what was going on in the hall but once again she was disappointed. It wasn't Nick who'd arrived but the couple who had bought David's old house and were now his neighbours, Tom and Mavis Roughley. Sam had appeared hot on their heels.

Abbie tried her best but it was an effort to concentrate as conversation flowed around the room. She kept waiting for the bell to ring again but by the time the meal was ready to be served there was still no sign of Nick.

She followed the others into the dining-room and quickly realised that there was no place set for him at the table as they all sat down. What had happened? Why had Nick decided not to come tonight after all? Had…had it anything to do with her being there?

'I believe you're a district nurse, Abbie?'

She forced down the sick feeling that Nick might be trying to avoid her as she turned to answer the question. Laura's brother, Adam Mackenzie, was staying with her for a few weeks, and they'd been seated next to each other. Now she fixed a smile to her mouth as she looked at him. He was very good-looking in a no-nonsense kind of way, with thick blond hair and bright blue eyes. Yet she found her heart aching because his wasn't the one face she wanted to see so much…

'That's right,' she replied quickly, before the silence lapsed into awkwardness. 'I've been doing the job almost four years now.'

'And you still enjoy it?' Adam continued, smiling at her as though he found her attractive. Abbie felt a little colour run up her face because it had been a long time since a man had looked at her with such interest. She wouldn't have been human if she hadn't been a little flattered.

'I do. It's everything I dreamt it would be. Oh, there are days—usually when it's pouring down with rain and I'm ankle-deep in mud at one of the farms—when I wonder why I left the hospital where I used to work, but it never lasts long,' she replied with a light laugh.

'Oh, so you worked in a hospital before?' Adam queried, tucking into the fresh pasta starter with evident relish.

'Mmm, at Bristol in the A and E department,' she answered, forking up a mouthful of the delicious pasta herself.

'Really?' He laughed deeply, his handsome face lighting up with amusement as he shot a glance along the table at his sister. 'I think Laura planned this deliberately, then, seating us together. We have something in common.'

'I'm sorry?' Abbie frowned as she wondered what he'd meant.

He gave her a warm smile. 'I specialise in advanced trauma life support. I actually lecture on the subject. My aim is to ensure that an ATLS module is built into the induction course to all A and E work, but it's an uphill struggle, trying to convince health authorities of the need for it.'

'I can imagine. Funding is probably the determining factor,' she replied, trying to keep her tone even. Was Laura doing a little matchmaking by seating her and Adam together—as he'd implied?

'Oh, undoubtedly! But we were talking about your work, Abbie. Tell me more about what you do.'

Adam's interest was genuine and, despite her unease about Laura's intentions, she found herself telling him about her work. It helped take her mind off Nick's absence, although that didn't mean the hurt had gone away. That Nick might have decided to avoid her after their run-in the other day was a bitter reminder of the distance between them.

'Right, if everyone has finished, I'll serve the pudding,' Laura announced as she stood up, creating a small gap in the conversation.

'Damn, I've forgotten to open the wine to go with it,' David declared, getting up to hurry from the room.

'Let me help you carry the dishes through,' Abbie offered immediately, helping Laura gather up the plates. She followed her to the kitchen and put them on the big pine table then looked around. 'This is beautiful! I love that stencilled border of pansies—did you do it?'

'Uh-huh…with a bit of help from Emily.' Laura stacked the plates in the dishwasher then went to the fridge and took out a huge glass bowl of fresh fruit salad. 'She loves anything that involves painting and getting herself generally messy!'

'I can imagine!' Abbie laughed as she collected bowls from the dresser and put them on the tray. 'Where is Emily at the moment?'

'Upstairs with her friend Kelly and little Chloe Jackson. She's having a sleep-over party, although I don't think there's going to be much sleeping!' Laura laughed as she added a jug of cream and a plate of melt-in-the-mouth shortcake biscuits to the assortment on the tray. 'Good job we converted the attic into a playroom so we can't hear the noise.'

'Wait until junior comes along. Then you'll know what noise is.' David had come in with the wine and was frantically hunting through the drawers.

'If you're looking for the corkscrew it's on top of the fridge,' Laura advised him. 'And don't be so smug. OK, so this is my first baby and I don't have your experience, but I think I can guess how noisy he or she is going to be!'

He kissed her quickly. 'I still think you're going to be in for a shock,' he said, winking at Abbie over the top of his wife's head. He laughed when Laura stuck her tongue out at him. 'Now, now, that will only promote bad habits…'

'Tough,' she retorted. 'Oh, by the way, Mike said to tell you that he'll be late back. He's gone into Kendal to see a film then he's having something to eat afterwards.'

'We hardly see him now he's passed his driving test,' David grumbled, finally winning his battle with the cork. 'He and Danny Shepherd seem to spend all weekend gadding about the countryside.'

'Oh, he isn't with Danny tonight.' Laura made a last check on the tray then went to pick it up.

'I'll take that,' David told her immediately. 'You take the wine. So, who is Mike out with, then?'

'Trisha. Mike's taken her to the cinema tonight,' Laura explained, picking up the bottle.

'As in a date?' David looked stunned and both Abbie and Laura laughed.

'Come as a surprise, has it, David?' she joked.

'Yes. I tend to forget Mike's *that* age!' he grimaced. 'I hope he's going to behave himself and act sensibly.'

'Oh, don't worry about that. Most teenagers could give us advice in a lot of areas. And Mike is sensible, just like his father,' Laura teased.

'Hmm, there's sensible and then there's *sensible*,' David replied. 'I'm not that old that I can't recall what it's like to be subjected to rampaging hormones!'

'I should hope not!' Laura retorted, patting her abdomen. 'I didn't manage this all by myself in case you've forgotten!'

The two women laughed as David hurriedly left the kitchen, looking rather pink.

'You're a dreadful tease, Laura,' Abbie chided.

'I know.' She sounded not at all abashed. 'So, how are you and Adam getting along? I thought you'd have something in common—that's why I sat you together.'

'He's very easy to talk to.' It was her turn to feel a little uncomfortable as she caught the speculative look Laura gave her.

'Very diplomatically put. In other words, it isn't love at first sight so don't go expecting too much—is that right?'

'Don't be silly. I'm sure you didn't intend…' Abbie groaned as she saw the expression on her face. 'You did, didn't you?'

'Of course. I'm sure Adam already guessed that because he knows me so well. And I've been singing your praises for his benefit ever since he got here.'

'I wish you hadn't. I…I'm not interested in an emotional involvement at the moment,' Abbie said quietly.

'I think you're making a mistake to rule out the possibility.' Laura sounded very sure of herself. She smiled as Abbie glanced at her in surprise. 'You have a lot of love to give, Abbie. You could make some lucky man very happy.'

She didn't say anything more as she took the wine into the dining-room. Abbie followed more slowly, thinking about what she'd said. Was she being a fool to rule out another relationship? Maybe she was. But surely it was better not to rush into anything for the wrong reasons? If and when she did commit herself again it would be to the man she loved. Next time she wouldn't settle for anything less!

It was a pleasant evening despite everything and Abbie enjoyed it. When Adam offered to walk her home, she accepted because there didn't seem any reason to refuse. It was a clear night, stars shining brightly in an almost cloud-less sky, the wind not cold enough to make the short walk to her house unpleasant.

They kept up an undemanding conversation as they walked along the high street. There were few cars about but one passed them just as they reached the end of her road. Abbie glanced at it and felt a shock of surprise hit her as she recognised Nick behind the wheel. He didn't acknowledge her in any way as he drove on, although she knew that he'd seen her, and her heart ached as she realised that her assumptions must have been correct. Nick obvi-ously wasn't ill so he must have changed his mind about attending the dinner party because he'd wanted to avoid her.

'Are you all right, Abbie?'

The concern in Adam Mackenzie's voice alerted her to the fact that she was still staring after the departing car. She quickly began walking again, fixing a smile to her mouth to disguise her hurt.

'Yes, fine. Sorry. I…I was just miles away, that's all.'

They reached her house and she turned to Adam and held out her hand. 'Thank you for walking me home—it was kind of you.'

'My pleasure, believe me. I enjoyed talking to you to-night, Abbie. Maybe we could go out for a drink some time. I'll be in the area for a couple of weeks so shall I give you a ring?' He took her hand and held it as he waited for her to answer.

She gave a small shrug, her heart aching so hard that it felt as though there was a lump of pain in the very centre of her. 'Why not? Thank you.'

'I'll speak to you soon, then.' He gave her a final smile and walked unhurriedly up the road. She let herself into the house, but instead of going to bed she went into the sitting-room and stood by the window. She closed her eyes as the memory of how Nick had looked at her so coldly before he'd driven away imprinted itself into her mind. Nothing had seemed to hurt quite so much...

'I was hoping I'd see you today, my dear.'

Mrs Delaney stopped her as she was leaving church the following morning. She'd been in two minds as to whether to go to the service because she felt so worn out. Another sleepless night had left dark shadows under her eyes and she saw the older woman look at her in concern.

'Are you feeling all right, Abbie? You look dreadfully tired.'

'I'm fine. Work's been a bit tough lately,' she excused herself, and heard Mrs Delaney sigh.

'Oh, dear, then I don't know if I should ask you what I was going to.'

'Is it something to do with Nick?' she guessed, moving aside so that other people could pass them.

'Yes. Who else?' Mrs Delaney took her arm. 'We may as well walk together as we're going the same way.'

'Isn't he feeling well?' Abbie asked, trying to quell a sudden rush of alarm at the thought.

'No. The muscle spasms seem to be increasing at the moment and I don't know what to do for the best,' the older woman admitted. 'Nick tries not to let me see how bad they are but I can always tell when he's in pain. Yesterday was particularly awful for him, which is why he couldn't go to the dinner party last night. He was in pain all day long so that by the time evening came he was worn out.'

'I thought I saw him in the car late last night,' Abbie commented, hating herself for the relief she felt that it hadn't been the thought of seeing her that had kept Nick away. Was it really better to think of him in pain? she chided herself. But it was a no-win situation and impossible to answer.

'Probably. He just needed to get out to take his mind off the whole wretched day. I really don't know what to do for the best, though.'

'Physiotherapy would help,' Abbie advised, trying to treat the matter professionally.

'That's why we had the pool cleaned out. When he was in hospital he found that the hydrotherapy sessions were marvellous for easing the spasms, but so far he hasn't made any attempt to use the pool.' Mrs Delaney took a deep breath. 'I wondered if you'd try to make him see sense, Abbie?'

'I'm not sure he'd pay any attention to me...' she began, but Mrs Delaney laughed.

'You're the only one Nick *does* pay attention to, believe me! He's been so much more positive since you spoke to him, my dear.'

Abbie blushed as she recalled the conversation Mrs Delaney had overheard. 'Well, I suppose I could try,' she offered hurriedly to cover her confusion.

'Thank you. The major and I have been invited out to tea this afternoon so that would be the perfect opportunity. You and Nick can have an hour or so on your own without any interruptions.' Mrs Delaney didn't give her time to object. 'Around three, then? Perfect.'

She was gone before Abbie could blink, leaving her reeling as she realised what she had let herself in for. She had the uncomfortable feeling that Nick wasn't going to be pleased to see her once he found out what she wanted!

Abbie rang the doorbell a fourth time, wondering if there had been a change of plans and nobody had thought to tell her. She'd been standing on the Delaneys' doorstep for a good five minutes now and so far there had been no answer.

'Yes…? Oh, it's you.'

Nick suddenly appeared around the side of the house, his face holding an expression which not even an optimist would have considered welcoming. Abbie struggled to contain the jumble of emotions she felt as he stared at her with hard blue eyes.

'What do you want, Abbie? Or should I guess?' His laughter was taunting and she felt one emotion surface at a rush above all the others. She could think of better ways to spend a Sunday afternoon than having him speak to her like that!

'Score one for astuteness,' she replied with an acerbity that wiped the mocking smile off his handsome face in an instant. Without the mask of amusement to disguise it, the lines of pain were all too obvious to see, and she felt her heart give a reluctant hiccup of sympathy which disappeared immediately as he continued in the same biting vein.

'So Mother has been interfering again, has she? I thought she was looking rather edgy before she left. I expect she persuaded you to come round to see if you could talk some sense into me.'

'Score two!' she shot back, folding her arms and regarding him with raised brows. 'Now, let's see if you can make it a hat trick by behaving as predictably as I expect you to. Any second now you're going to tell me that you don't want my help and that I've wasted my time. Well, save your breath, Nick, because I'm going home.'

She turned to leave then came up short as she found him in front of her. He glared at her with angry blue eyes, a rim of colour edging his cheek-bones.

'You may as well. I'm sure you have better ways to spend your free time than being here with me, and someone better to spend it with!' he snapped back.

Her head spun as she heard the naked emotion in his voice. Nick was jealous? He couldn't be! She tried to tell herself that she'd imagined it but one glimpse of the expression on his face was all the proof she needed. But what did he have to be jealous of...or, rather, who?

Her mind made the quantum leap and she almost gasped out loud. Nick had seen her with Adam Mackenzie last night and had obviously put two and two together. Fair enough, but it was the reason why his maths had gone so far off course which made her heart race. If Nick cared nothing about her, why should he care who she'd been with?

'There are certainly people who would welcome my company more than you apparently do,' she said softly, watching his face while her heart raced almost out of control.

'I'm sure there are. So, off you go, Abbie. Don't let me keep you.' He swung the chair round but not before she'd seen the pain which darkened his eyes. It was the reason for it that had her following as he made his way swiftly round to the back garden. A ramp had been built alongside the steps leading into the glass-enclosed poolhouse and he propelled himself up it and in through the open doors. He stopped on the tiled deck area at the deep end of the pool then looked at her again.

'You still here? I thought you'd be on your way home now that you've done your duty,' he snapped as he unzipped his sweatsuit jacket and peeled it off. Tossing it onto the floor, he set to work on the sweatsuit bottoms, struggling a little as he tried to work them down over his hips and thighs while he sat in the chair.

Abbie clenched her fists to stop herself going to help him because she knew that was a sure way to make matters worse. Instead, she watched silently as he finally divested himself of his outer clothing so that he was left wearing only navy blue swimming shorts.

In a fast sweep her eyes travelled over his body, taking

note of the powerful muscles in his torso, the long, tanned legs which still looked as though they could bear his weight. Her gaze came back to his face and she felt her heart contract as she saw the uncertainty in his eyes and understood the reason for it. Did Nick really believe that his helplessness would disgust her?

He held her gaze for a moment then looked away, a flush of colour running up his neck. 'I suppose Mother told you about yesterday,' he asked in a quieter tone.

'Yes. She also told me that you hadn't made any use of the pool so far.'

He shrugged, the muscles in his shoulders flexing beneath his tanned skin. 'I've been waiting for the right opportunity.' He must have sensed that she didn't understand because he continued flatly, 'I wasn't sure if I could manage getting in and out of the pool by myself. I preferred to test it out when I was on my own.'

'But that's crazy, Nick! What would have happened if you'd got stuck and there was no one around to help you?' she protested. 'It was such a risk to take…'

'Not much of a risk. I haven't that much to lose, have I?'

It was said so starkly that her eyes misted with tears. She knelt down beside him, not trying to hide how she felt. 'Don't say that, Nick. It isn't true!'

'Isn't it?' His tone gentled as he reached out and lifted a glistening tear from her long lashes. 'Tears, Abbie? I'm flattered that you care that much.'

'Of course I care! Damn you, Nick, don't you dare think of doing anything so stupid as swimming by yourself ever again. Promise me!' She wasn't aware that she was gripping his hands until she felt his fingers close around hers and grip them back. Her breath caught as she felt the surge of electricity which shot through her fingertips before Nick let her go with a speed that told her that he wasn't immune to its power either.

'All right, I promise. So, as you're here to act as life-guard, I'll see how I get on, shall I?' he said with an attempt at lightness. Abbie summoned a smile but it wasn't easy when every cell in her body was humming from the charge it had just received.

'I suppose so. Although I'd be happier if I was in there with you.'

'There are spare costumes in the changing-room if you want to come in,' he offered. He grinned as she hesitated. 'Afraid I'll duck you?'

She laughed at his teasing, glad that his sombre mood had lifted. 'You and whose army? Give me five minutes and then we'll see who gets ducked!'

'Don't forget you're dealing with an injured man, Nurse Fraser,' he advised, trying to sound suitably helpless and failing miserably. She let her eyes roam over his powerful body then hurried away without letting slip the retort which was on the tip of her tongue. Even with the wheelchair very much in evidence Nick looked far from helpless, to her mind!

It took her a few minutes to find a costume that fitted her, although the style left a lot to be desired! The pool hadn't been used for many years and most of the costumes hanging in the cabin were rather past their sell-by date. However, a plain one-piece suit in deep blue seemed appropriate enough so she quickly slipped out of her clothes and put it on, trying not to let her self-consciousness show as Nick's eyes travelled over her body as she approached him.

She'd filled out since they'd last gone swimming together, and her hips and bust were fuller than they had been, yet there was nothing other than a very masculine appreciation in his gaze as he studied her. However, he made no comment as he positioned the chair beside the pool and prepared to slip into the water.

'Let me go first,' she offered, sliding into the water ahead of him. It was deep and she hung onto the side as Nick performed a sitting dive into the water then broke the surface several yards away. He struck out in a gentle breast-stroke at first, using his upper body to propel him through the water and letting its buoyancy support his useless limbs.

Abbie swam over to join him but by the time they'd done two laps he was way ahead of her.

'You're too good for me,' she admitted, gasping for breath as she trod water while he began another lap. He stopped at the end of the pool, clinging to the rail as he grinned triumphantly at her.

'Out of condition, that's your problem,' he taunted.

'Why, you cheeky thing…' Using the flat of her hand, she scooped water towards him and laughed as he got a good soaking. 'That'll teach you… Nick… Nick!' Her voice reached a high-pitched screech as he suddenly disappeared beneath the water and came up alongside her. It was obvious what he intended and she let out another scream as she turned and frantically began swimming away from him.

He caught up with her in a couple of strokes, his hard, muscular arms closing around her body as he twisted her round to face him. 'Revenge is very sweet, so they say…'

'No! Don't! Please…' She gripped his shoulders, meaning to push him away and prevent the threatened ducking, only as soon as her hands encountered his slickly smooth skin she forgot what she was doing. He felt so wonderful, she thought wonderingly, so smooth and hard and strong…

Her face lifted to his and she felt her breath catch as she saw the expression in his eyes, the same sense of wonderment she was feeling, the same deep yearning and need.

'Nick…' His name was the softest of whispers so that

afterwards she wasn't sure that she'd said it out loud. Not that it mattered, of course, because they'd never needed words to communicate and they didn't need them now…

He made a sound deep in his throat, almost a moan, before his mouth found hers and it was lost in that first urgent contact. His lips were cool from the water yet the fire beneath the chill scorched her. She wrapped her arms around his neck and opened her mouth as his tongue probed her lips, clinging to him as they slowly sank, their bodies entwined.

She closed her eyes as the water lapped over their heads, holding onto him as though her life depended on it as they drifted down in a dizzying spiral, before slowly floating back to the surface, still entwined.

Nick gripped the edge of the pool as they broke the surface, his face deeply flushed, his eyes glittering with a desire she would have needed to be blind not to see. He still had one arm tightly around her and Abbie gasped as their hips brushed so that she could feel the hardness of his body pressing against hers.

Her eyes flew to his face as he gave a husky laugh, so deeply sensual that her bones seemed to melt as she heard it. 'Seems as though something is functioning all right.'

'It…it seems like that,' she stammered, flushing hotly as she looked away. What had happened had caught them both off guard and her mind was still reeling. But somehow she had to find the strength to be sensible before things got out of hand. 'Nick, I—'

'No. Don't spoil it. Not yet… Not yet!' His mouth was even more urgent as he kissed her again, pressing her back against the side of the pool so that she could feel the coldness of the tiles all down her spine. The contrast with the heat of his powerful body against her front was so extreme that she shivered convulsively while all thoughts of being sensible melted away. She wanted him to kiss her—wanted

to recapture the magic they'd once shared, if only for this
brief time!

She clung to his shoulders as the kiss ran on and on. He
didn't touch her because he needed his hands to hold onto
the rail and keep himself afloat. She was glad. It was almost
unbearably stimulating, just feeling his body brushing hers
as they drifted together as the water lapped against the side
of the pool. Anything more would have been too much
when already it felt as though she were drowning in sensations, drowning in desire, drowning in her love for him...

She must have made some sound as the thought slid into
her mind without any warning because he drew back
abruptly. His handsome face was set into a frown as he
stared at her with eyes so dark they appeared almost black.
'What is it, Abbie? Tell me what's wrong.'

CHAPTER SIX

'I…' ABBIE had no idea what she'd been going to say when a voice suddenly shouted from outside.

'Hello. Anyone there?'

They both swung round as they heard footsteps coming up the steps. When James suddenly appeared she didn't know whether to laugh or cry in relief at having been spared answering the question. Nick gave her a last searching look before he turned and swam to the other end of the pool.

'Hi, there. To what do we owe this honour?' he asked lightly, giving no indication that he regretted the interruption.

'I wanted a word with you, Nick, but maybe this isn't the best time. I wondered if Abbie was here in a professional capacity when I saw her car, but obviously not,' he added with a grin.

'Oh, I wouldn't say that.' Nick's tone was as bland as the look he gave her but there was a wicked gleam in his eyes. 'She's certainly managed to make me feel better since she got here.'

She turned away, not wanting him to see the heat that flooded her face. Maybe Nick could treat what had happened lightly but she couldn't! She swam to the steps and climbed out of the water, avoiding looking at either of the men. 'I…I'm going to get changed.'

'There should be towels in the changing-room, Abbie,' Nick called after her, but she did no more than nod, before hurrying away. Closing the door behind her, she leaned against it as her legs threatened to give way. Her head was reeling both from Nick's kisses and her own devastating thoughts.

Was she in love with him? Could it be true? Or was her mind playing tricks, echoes of the past coming back to haunt the present with emotions as ephemeral as the dreams which had haunted her for years?

It was impossible to tell while she was in such turmoil, but somehow she had to get her feelings about Nick straight in her own head. Not that she imagined he'd have any such difficulty. His recent engagement was proof that his heart belonged to another woman. Although he might have felt desire for her just now, that was all it had been—nothing more!

It took some time to towel herself dry and change into her clothes again and she didn't hurry. When she left the changing-room there was no sign of Nick in the pool so she could only assume that James had helped him get out.

She hesitated, tempted to slip away without saying good-bye, but in the end decided that would only provoke questions she wasn't prepared to answer just yet. Until she understood how she really felt about Nick she had to carry on as though nothing had changed.

She finally tracked him and James down to the kitchen where the kettle was boiling away for tea. She took over the task of making it then carried the pot over to the table along with some mugs.

'Thanks.' Nick's expression was impossible to read as he looked up at her with hooded eyes yet she felt the colour run up her cheeks. It sounded crazy but she knew he was thinking about what had happened between them in the pool just a few minutes previously.

'I…I've forgotten the milk,' she stammered, hurrying to the fridge and getting out a fresh pint bottle, but her hands were shaking as she filled the jug. She closed her eyes, trying to blot out the seductive memory of those kisses they'd shared, but it was impossible to drive them from her mind. Nick had kissed her with such desire that surely he must feel something for her? she reasoned. But it didn't mean he was in love with her, her busy mind countered.

'So, what did you want to see me about, James?' Nick asked as she took the milk jug to the table and set about pouring the tea.

'I needed some advice. And you're the best-qualified person to give it to me. Thanks.' James accepted the cup Abbie placed in front of him.

'Has this something to do with Adrian Shaw?' she guessed, glad to have something to take her mind off her own problems.

'Yes. Have you spoken to Nick about him yet?' James asked, sipping the hot tea.

'I...I haven't had time,' she replied, avoiding Nick's eyes as she saw him glance at her. He was dressed once more in the black sweatsuit, his dark hair clinging wetly to his skull. He'd obviously showered away the chlorinated pool water and the spicy tang of the soap he'd used was a delicate stimulant to senses already too highly tuned. When he reached for his cup his arm brushed her hip and she couldn't stop herself from jumping at the contact.

She took a deep breath as she sat down, willing her jangling nerves to quieten, but all it took was the husky sound of his deep voice to set them off again. The trouble was that every bit of her was still so attuned to him that it was near impossible to break the spell.

'This is linked to what we were discussing the other night in the Fleece?' he asked quietly.

'Yes. I'm becoming increasingly concerned about Adrian, to be frank,' James replied. He swiftly outlined everything that had happened recently, then continued, 'I had a word with Harry and Rose but they refuse to admit that anything might be wrong with the boy. As far as they're concerned, Adrian is completely better and that's the end of the story.'

'But you don't agree? And neither does Abbie?' Nick shot her a searching look and she shook her head. 'You're right to be concerned, both of you. Only about thirty per cent of schizophrenics ever return to leading a normal life. The majority need constant care and support and there'll always be some sort of impairment in their behaviour. Is Adrian still taking his medication, do you know?'

'That's one of the things I asked Harry but he was very evasive. I got the impression that he didn't believe it was still necessary,' James replied, sounding worried.

'It could be that he suspects his son isn't taking it and is afraid to promote a confrontation. A lot of relatives have difficulty in dealing with an often volatile situation,' Nick advised, thoughtfully stirring sugar into his tea. 'By the very nature of their illness, schizophrenics are often easily upset and hard to handle, especially for anyone emotionally involved with them.'

'I *did* wonder if that was a problem. I'm glad I wasn't so far off track, although it doesn't help.' James sighed. 'What do you suggest, Nick? Something needs to be done.'

'Obviously the boy must be encouraged to continue taking his medication—that's imperative at this stage,' he replied firmly.

'But it can't be easy, persuading someone to take medication if they really don't want to,' Abbie cut in.

He grimaced. 'It isn't. I think the best way forward in this situation is to talk to the boy's parents again and make them understand that they aren't helping their son by taking this line. Then you can offer them support. It might help if you saw Adrian on a daily basis, Abbie, and took over the task of supervising his medication. It's often easier for an outsider to do that.'

'Of course,' she agreed at once, then sighed. 'Although

I don't know how Adrian will feel about me interfering. When I spoke to him the other day he was extremely wary of me. He asked me if ''they'' had sent me, although I don't know who he meant.'

'It could have been his parents he was referring to. Or, more worryingly, it could have been because he's already suffering delusions, one of the main symptoms of the illness,' Nick explained grimly.

'Hearing voices and feeling persecuted—it isn't uncommon, I believe,' James put in, sounding equally concerned.

'It isn't. And it's very worrying if that's the case here. My advice to you, James, is to get on to Adrian's psychiatrist and see what he advises. It could be that he'll want to see the boy again to assess him.'

'I'll do that. Thanks, Nick. I'm glad we had time to discuss this. I was meaning to have a word with you last night but you didn't show up,' James replied.

'Oh, it was one of those days.' Nick brushed aside the reason for his absence from the dinner. 'I was sorry to miss the party, though. Did you have a good time?'

James laughed. 'We most certainly did! I have to confess that I was a little worse for wear this morning!' He turned to Abbie with a smile. 'I was glad that Adam offered to walk you home. Elizabeth and I were going to drop you off but we ended up leaving the car at David's and walking back. Still, you and Adam seemed to be getting along extremely well so I don't suppose you were all that bothered.'

The teasing note in his voice was unmistakable and Abbie felt her face grow warm. She muttered something but James failed to take the hint and let the matter drop. 'I imagine you and Adam had a lot in common, with you having worked in A and E before coming here?'

'Er…yes. He seems a very nice man,' she added lamely, avoiding looking in Nick's direction.

'I believe you know him, Nick?' James continued. 'Laura mentioned that you two were friends.'

'More acquaintances, to be honest,' he replied smoothly, his tone giving away little about his feelings. If he was at all troubled by the subject of Adam Mackenzie then it certainly didn't show, Abbie thought. So much for thinking that he might have been jealous. It just proved how wrong she'd been!

She jumped as she suddenly realised that both men were looking expectantly at her. 'I'm sorry, what was that?'

'I was just asking if Adam was staying in the area very long,' Nick said in that same smooth tone, which suddenly annoyed her intensely.

'He mentioned something about being around for a few weeks,' she replied coolly.

'Then, when you see him again, maybe you'd ask him to give me a call. It would be good to catch up on what's been happening.' His look was as bland as a judge's yet she knew very well what he was doing. It infuriated her! If Nick wanted to know if she'd arranged to see Adam Mackenzie again, why didn't he ask?

'I'll certainly do that,' she agreed, getting up so fast that her chair scraped against the red quarry tiles with a horrible grating noise. 'Anyway, I'd better be on my way now. I'll see you tomorrow, James, I expect.'

She gave them both a tight little smile, her eye skimming over Nick's face without meeting his eyes. Maybe it wouldn't have annoyed her quite so much if she'd thought he cared about her seeing Adam again, but his tone had made it plain that he couldn't give two hoots what she did. At least it answered the question of what had been behind those kisses…simple masculine lust, triggered by the closeness of an available and *willing* female!

'Thanks for coming, Abbie.'

She was almost at the door when he spoke and she

couldn't help glancing back. He was cradling the cup in one long-fingered hand, his face holding an expression that started up the turmoil all over again. Was that real anguish she could see in his eyes or was she imagining it?

She took a quick breath but it didn't dispel the confusion. 'That's all right, Nick. I…I enjoyed the swim and everything.'

She only realised how he might interpret that statement when he gave her a wickedly intimate smile. 'Oh, so did I, Abbie. So did I.'

She spun round and headed out of the door so fast that it was a wonder she didn't leave a vapour trail in her wake! What James thought of her hasty departure she had no idea. She drove home, trying her hardest to make sense of everything that had gone on that afternoon but it was impossible. Until she knew how she really felt about Nick then nothing was going to make much sense in her life.

'Calling him William… Oh, hi, Abbie. I was just saying that Sophie Jackson had her baby last night—a little boy, eight pounds three ounces and I believe she's calling him William.'

'Why, that's brilliant news!' Abbie smiled in delight as Elizabeth greeted her with the news. It was Monday morning and she was a little late arriving at the surgery for the weekly meeting. She'd had difficulty sleeping as her mind had spun in endless circles. She'd finally dropped off in the early hours of the morning then had missed the alarm.

She tossed her coat over a chair then gratefully accepted the mug of coffee Sam thrust into her hands. 'Oh, do I need this! I overslept and didn't have time for a cup of coffee before I left home.'

'Out on the tiles, were you, Nurse Fraser?' he teased, grinning at her. 'Could it be that you and the handsome Dr

Mackenzie decided to pick up where you left off on Saturday night?'

'No, it couldn't! For your information, O'Neill, I was at home by myself all last night,' she retorted. She turned to Elizabeth again, not wanting him to pursue the subject—as he was quite capable of doing. She was rather sensitive about the subject of Adam Mackenzie mainly because she was still trying to understand Nick's response.

Had he been jealous? she wondered for the umpteenth time, then sighed. How on earth could she decide that when she couldn't make up her mind how *she* felt about anything any more? 'So, what happened about Sophie? She was due to have the baby in hospital, wasn't she?'

'Yes, and it all went as planned. Her mother called me out when she started having contractions and I stayed with her until the ambulance arrived. William was born not long after they got to hospital, and it was a straightforward delivery with no complications,' Elizabeth explained.

'Sophie will be staying in hospital for five days then will come home. The midwife is going on holiday so you'll need to take over Sophie's care for a week or so, Abbie.'

'That's fine. I'll make a note of it in my diary. Oh, before I forget, I don't need to see Trisha Shepherd any more. She's managed to overcome her fear of giving herself the injections and is coping extremely well.'

'That's great! Well done. It'll be so much easier for her from now on,' Elizabeth enthused.

'Talking of Trisha, that's just reminded me of something Mike told me on Saturday night,' David put in. 'You know that he and Trisha went into Kendal? Well, when he took her home Adrian Shaw was hanging around outside her house. Mike said that it was really odd because Adrian didn't say anything but just stood there, staring at them. Evidently, Trisha was a bit scared. She said that she thinks Adrian's following her.'

'We were only talking to Nick Delaney about this very problem yesterday, weren't we, Abbie?' James responded. 'He advised me to get on to the boy's psychiatrist. I'll give him a ring later on today.'

'Good. At least that's in hand, although we must keep a close watch on the situation,' David said thankfully before he suddenly grinned. 'And now to a more cheerful subject, folks. The new computer is being delivered on Wednesday and we should be up and running...barring gremlins...by the end of the week. I take it that we're all in favour of Abbie's suggestion?'

'I might be if I knew what you were talking about,' Elizabeth grumbled. However, after Abbie quickly outlined her idea about holding a launching party she was full of enthusiasm. 'I think it's a great idea! We'll have an open evening, lay on cheese and wine and show everyone what the new system can do. We just need to agree on a date.'

After a lot of cross-referencing of diaries, it was finally decided to hold the launch in three weeks' time, which would give them chance to come to grips with the new technology. The meeting broke up after that and everyone hurried away to get ready for surgery.

Abbie collected her list of calls for the day and made her way out to her car. She was just opening the door when another car turned into the car park and her heart skipped a couple of beats as she realised it was Nick. He parked beside her, rolling down the window so he could speak to her.

'Are you just on your way out?'

'Yes. I've a fairly easy day for once—eight calls and only two any distance away,' she told him, striving to match his casual tone. 'What are you doing here so early, anyway?'

'I decided to pop in to see James before the rush. I've been thinking more about Adrian Shaw and thought it might help if I looked through his case notes. Obviously, it would be unprofessional of me to interfere when he's under someone else's care, but I thought it might help if I made a few suggestions,' he explained.

'I'm sure James would be grateful,' she said at once. 'He was just saying that he intends to get in touch with Adrian's psychiatrist today.'

'Good. That's the first step.' Nick opened the car door. 'Would you give me a hand, Abbie? If you could lift the chair out…?'

'Of course.' She quickly lifted the lightweight wheelchair from the car. It took Nick only a few minutes to get himself comfortably settled in it. 'You're getting good at this,' she observed brightly, thinking suddenly how tired he looked now that the sunlight was playing over his face.

'It's a skill I'd prefer not to develop, but I don't have much choice,' he replied flatly, looking up at her with shadowed blue eyes. 'About yesterday, Abbie. I wanted to apologise.'

'Apologise?' she repeated blankly.

'For what happened in the pool. I appreciate you coming to see me and I'm only sorry that I allowed things to get out of hand.'

'Th-that's all right,' she replied, her heart seeming to break as a fierce pain lanced through it. Nick obviously regretted what had happened and it hurt to realise that he preferred to brush it aside with an apology. She'd been right to suspect that it had been nothing more than an instinctive response to her nearness which had triggered the whole incident.

She bade him a quick goodbye and got into her car as he headed for the surgery. Not that she could see him. The tears which clouded her vision blinded her to everything but the truth. That was painfully clear. Those kisses which had meant so much to her had meant nothing to him!

CHAPTER SEVEN

ABBIE arrived at Yewthwaite Farm just before lunch. One of the farm workers had been feeling off colour for a couple of weeks, and blood tests had shown that he was suffering from Q fever. She'd been monitoring his progress on a twice-weekly basis.

Harvey Walsh, who owned the farm, came to meet her as she drew up. A pleasant man in his early forties, he'd been very concerned that the new farm worker had contracted the disease from his stock. Harvey's farm was the biggest in the area and he prided himself on his good management of his animals.

'Come to see Len again, have you?' he asked as Abbie got out of the car.

'Yes. How's he doing?' she asked, lifting her case from the back. Q fever began with influenza-like symptoms which progressed to a form of pneumonia if left untreated, as had happened in this case. Len Parker had been quite ill and the main worry now was that hepatitis might develop despite the course of antibiotics he was on.

'I'd say he was a bit better today.' Harvey led the way from the yard toward the tied cottage where Len lived. 'I had the vet out here and he's tested my stock but he can't find any trace of the infection. He thinks Len must have caught it at his last place of work so he's contacting the farm to advise them.'

'It's more than likely. Len's only been with you five weeks now, hasn't he? There's usually a gap of roughly twenty days between infection and the first signs of the illness. If there are infected animals on the last farm Len

93

worked at then the farmer needs to take adequate precautions. You can contract Q fever just by inhaling contaminated dust,' she explained as they reached the cottage.

'Aye, so the vet said. Anyway, come up to the house after you've finished here and have a bite to eat,' Harvey said.

'Thank you. I'll be there as soon as I've checked Len over.' She accepted with real pleasure. One of the main joys of her job, she thought as she rapped on the cottage door, was dealing with such lovely people.

Len was feeling a little better that day, as Harvey had said. The course of tetracycline he'd been prescribed was evidently working.

'I only wish I'd had the sense to go to the doctor when I first felt poorly,' he said, coughing a little, 'then maybe I wouldn't have been so ill. I just thought it was a touch of flu, like, so took no notice.'

'It's an easy mistake to make,' Abbie said soothingly. 'I don't suppose you wanted to take time off work, having just started a new job.'

'That I didn't. But Mr Walsh has been very good, I'll give him that. A lot of folk would have had me out on my ear by now. One of the reasons we came here was so the wife could be near to her family, you see. Her mother's getting on now and her dad's not all that good on his feet.'

'Oh, I didn't realise. Where does your wife's family live?' she asked, writing her findings down on Len's card.

'Newthwaite. We're handy here for seeing them, which is why I took this job,' Len explained. 'Things have been a bit difficult lately because Mary was made redundant. She's a physiotherapist but there'd been some sort of cuts made to the hospital's budget and they had to get rid of staff. We'd been talking about moving up here for ages and it seemed the best time to do it. Mary's hoping to get another job but she's not had any luck so far.

'We've been worried sick that I'd get the push from here, but Mr Walsh told me just to concentrate on getting better so I feel a lot easier in my mind.'

'Harvey Walsh is a nice man,' Abbie agreed. 'He won't go back on his word. So long as you play fair with him he'll treat you properly. Anyway, I'll see you in a couple of days' time, Len. But, so far as I'm concerned, it won't be long before you're up and about again.'

The kitchen door was on the latch when she went to the farmhouse. She gave a perfunctory knock then went in, knowing there was no need to stand on ceremony. Helen Walsh was just lifting a brimming dish of hotpot out of the oven and Abbie sniffed appreciatively.

'How did you know that I didn't have time for breakfast this morning?' she demanded as she put down her bag.

'Then you should do justice to this. Sit yourself down and I'll dish up.' Helen set about serving the meal, moving quickly and competently around the kitchen. Abbie watched her, thinking how well she looked. Helen had been recently diagnosed with MS but there certainly didn't appear to be much wrong with her at the moment.

'You're looking really well, Helen,' she observed as the other woman carried the plates to the table.

'I feel well!' Helen laughed. 'Oh, I know I still have MS and that the symptoms could come back tomorrow, but I've decided to take it one day at a time, as Dr O'Neill suggested.'

'I'm so glad,' Abbie said sincerely. 'I know that Dr O'Neill was really worried about you at one stage.'

'We're both grateful for all the support he's given us, aren't we, Harvey?' Helen said, looking around as her husband came into the room.

'We are, that. He's a first-rate doctor and I bet we aren't the only folk round here who are pleased he won't be going to Africa just yet awhile,' Harvey stated, going to the sink to wash his hands.

'That's a fact. Isn't it lovely about him and young Holly getting engaged? I believe they're both going to go overseas once she qualifies in a couple of years time,' Helen said.

'That's right.' Abbie hid her smile. It never failed to amaze her how quickly news spread around the town.

'Well, let's hope they decide to come back here afterwards, then,' Helen concluded. 'Now, tuck in, both of you. There's baked apples and custard for afters.'

'Oh, I'll need to go on a diet after this!' Abbie groaned, not needing much encouragement to set to work on the delicious food.

'There's hardly a pick on you!' Harvey declared with typical male insouciance, then looked surprised when she and Helen laughed.

They kept up a steady flow of conversation about local events as they ate. Abbie told them about the new computer and explained the merits of the video link to the hospital, which would mean that some patients would be able to speak to a consultant without travelling further than the surgery. Both Helen and Harvey were enthusiastic about the idea.

'Nice to know that we're moving with the times even here,' Helen observed, opening the oven to take out the apples, which were brimming with melted brown sugar and spices. 'It might help attract some new blood into the town. Too many young people end up leaving because there aren't the opportunities here for them. Talking of which, who was that good-looking young man we saw you with the other night, Abbie? Harvey took me for a drink and we happened to see you walking home.'

'Oh, that was Laura's brother, Adam Mackenzie.' Abbie tried to hide her surprise. 'We'd been to Laura and David's housewarming do and he offered to walk me home afterwards.'

'Hmm, did he, indeed? Do I scent a hint of romance in the air, I wonder?' Helen teased as she put the bowls on the table.

'I very much doubt it!' Abbie laughed off the question but it made her uncomfortable all the same. Mention of Adam had naturally stirred up memories of Nick's reaction to seeing them together. Why *had* he appeared upset when he'd stated categorically only that morning that he was sorry about what had gone on in the pool yesterday?

The question haunted her for the rest of the day so that by the time she arrived home that evening she was worn out with thinking about it. She wasn't really hungry after such a big lunch so she just made herself a cup of tea and ate a couple of digestive biscuits with it. She'd just finished when the phone rang, and she went to answer it.

'Abbie? It's Adam Mackenzie here. How are you?'

'Fine, thanks. And you?' she replied, her heart sinking as she realised that he must be calling to invite her out. She didn't want to offend him but she wasn't sure that she wanted to go.

'I was wondering if you'd like to come for a drink tonight?' he asked, as expected.

'Well…' Her hesitation was obvious and she heard him laugh ruefully.

'Don't tell me—you're washing your hair?'

She had to laugh at his wry use of the age-old excuse. 'No, I'm not.'

'Then, please, say yes. I'm at a bit of a loose end, to be honest, and I could do with some company,' he said persuasively.

She hesitated only a moment longer but there was no real reason for her to refuse. And surely it would be better than sitting at home, worrying over problems she couldn't solve? 'All right, then. I'd love to come. Thank you.'

'Great! I'll pick you up round eight if that's OK.'

He hung up as soon as she'd agreed. Abbie put the phone down and immediately started wondering if she'd done the right thing. And why not? She was a free agent and owed no one an explanation about what she did.

She caught a glimpse of herself in the mirror on the wall and turned away as she saw the bleakness in her eyes. The simple truth was that when it came down to it nobody really cared one way or the other what she did—and that included Nick Delaney!

By the time Adam dropped her off at home Abbie was glad that she'd agreed to go out with him. He was an interesting companion who'd kept her entertained with stories about his work without monopolising the conversation. He'd made no secret of the fact that he found her attractive either, and it was like a small salve to her ego. Nick might not be interested in her but that didn't mean other men took the same view!

She hung up her jacket and was heading up to bed when she noticed that the message light on the answering machine was flashing. Frowning, she pressed the button and felt her heart turn over as she recognised Mrs Delaney's voice, asking her to ring as soon as she got in.

She quickly dialled the number, her heart racing as a dozen possibilities ran through her head. Had Nick been taken ill? Had there been another accident even?

The line was engaged and remained that way when she tried it two or three more times. She looked around, wondering what to do, but there wasn't any choice. She couldn't spend the night worrying about what had happened.

It took only a few minutes to drive to the Delaneys'

house, and her fear intensified when she saw David's car outside. Mrs Delaney answered the door, looking very grey and drawn.

'Oh, Abbie! Thank you for coming but everything seems to be all right now, I'm glad to say.'

'Is it Nick?' she demanded, stepping into the hall.

'Yes. He was in such terrible pain. He took some of the painkillers they'd given him at the hospital but they didn't help. I phoned Dr Ross when I couldn't get hold of you to ask your advice, although Nick didn't want me to.'

'You did the right thing, Mrs Delaney,' Abbie said comfortingly, looking round as David appeared. 'How is he?'

'A lot better now. I've given him an injection of dantrolene to control the pain and he's resting,' he explained.

'Can I see him?' she asked quickly.

'Yes, although he may be a bit sleepy. Anyway, I'll speak to you tomorrow, Abbie. Nick's been overdoing things today, which is probably what caused the problem tonight. He needs physiotherapy on a regular basis so we'll have to see what we can work out,' David told her.

'Of course.' She left him having a final word with Mrs Delaney as she hurried across the hall and quietly opened the bedroom door. A lamp had been left on beside the bed and she could see how worn out Nick looked as she crossed the room. He had his eyes closed and she thought he was asleep at first until he suddenly spoke.

'I suppose Mother rang you.'

'Yes. She was worried about you, Nick,' she replied softly, looking down at him anxiously. Sweat had dampened his hair so that a thick lock lay limply across his forehead. Without stopping to think, she brushed it back then felt a sharp stab of pain bite into her as he quickly turned his head away.

'Don't! I'd have thought the Florence Nightingale act

would have grown a bit boring by now. I'm surprised you came.'

His tone was as acerbic as the expression in his eyes as he suddenly opened them. It was obvious that he didn't want her there and his rejection hurt.

'There was a message on my answering machine when I got in, asking me to call your mother,' she stated flatly. 'The line was busy when I tried to phone her back so I drove over here.'

'I'm flattered. But I hope you didn't cut short your evening on my account, Abbie. Whatever will Adam think about you rushing off to minister to another man? It was him you were out with, I imagine?' His laughter was harsh as he saw her discomfort. 'I thought so. Still, I'm sure he'll understand when you explain that I'm just someone you feel sorry for.'

'Have you any idea how *boring* it is to keep going over the same old ground?' Her tone was almost as sharp as his had been. She gave a taunting little laugh, her temper rising inch by red-hot inch up the scale. 'How many times do I have to tell you that I don't feel sorry for you, Nick? It's the people who have to deal with you I reserve my sympathy for! Fortunately, I'm not one of them—'

'No! Damn you, Abbie, don't you dare go!' he snapped as she turned to leave.

'Why not? Give me one good reason why I should stay here and have you speak to me like that?' she demanded, staring at him with hard grey eyes so that she saw the grimace he suddenly gave.

'Because I don't really mean to be such a crashing boor,' he admitted with painful honesty.

'No? Well, you're making a first-class job of it!' she shot back, refusing to be mollified.

He gave an uncomfortable smile. 'I know. The worst thing is that I can see myself acting like a thirty-three-year-old toddler having a tantrum and yet I can't stop it happening!'

She laughed at the rueful note in his voice. 'At least you've got the description right.'

'I don't think I could forget it! It's just that—' He stopped abruptly and shook his head. 'It doesn't matter.'

'Of course it does. Tell me what you were going to say, Nick,' she said persuasively, sensing that this was important to him.

'It's just that nobody has any idea how it feels.' He closed his eyes and she saw him swallow. 'Have you any conception of what it does to a man to know that he's as helpless as a newborn babe?'

'No, I don't expect I have. So why don't you tell me, Nick?' Her tone gentled as she sat on the edge of the bed. 'All I want is to help you any way I can.'

'Why? Why bother with me, Abbie, when I end up pushing you away all the time?' His tone was rueful as he opened his eyes and looked at her.

'Because I'm aiming for sainthood?' She gave a gentle laugh, knowing instinctively that it was better to keep things light. 'Or maybe I'm just a glutton for punishment.'

He grimaced. 'Don't say that! I'm not trying to punish you, sweetheart.'

The endearment slipped out without him realising it but she felt the small thrill which ran through her at once. She looked down at her hands, willing herself not to betray how she felt. It had been such a long time since anyone had called her that, such a long time since Nick had used that term to her…

'If I'm punishing anyone then it's myself because I hate the way I am,' he continued, gaining her attention once more.

'But that's silly!' She didn't stop to think, before covering his hands with hers.

'Is it? I want to be able to do all the things I used to do, like going for a walk, getting into the car and driving off without it being a major operation.' He took a deep breath, his fingers closing around hers so tightly that they hurt. 'I want to be what I was, Abbie, not what I am now—just a broken shell!'

'I understand that, Nick. But it isn't possible…not yet. Maybe in time…' She stopped as she saw his face close up. He wouldn't allow himself to look to the future and she understood that feeling so well. Maybe it would help if she told him that.

'I know it's hard,' she said softly. 'It's natural to look back and think ''if only'' but it doesn't alter the situation. When…when Megan died I did the same. I kept thinking what might have happened if I'd done this or that, wondering if it would have changed things.'

'But it wouldn't have?' he asked softly.

'No.'

'What happened to her, Abbie?' His tone was as gentle as a summer breeze and so tender that tears sprang to her eyes.

She looked away, concentrating on their hands which were still linked together on top of the covers. 'It was a cot death. I put her to bed one night and she was dead when I went into her room the next morning.'

'It must have been a nightmare for you.' Nick's tone echoed with pain.

'It was. I spent months thinking back over the last few days of her life, trying to remember if there had been any warning signs, but there weren't any. Megan was well and happy when she went to sleep. She…she just never woke up again. I miss her so much, Nick, even now.'

Her tears started to flow freely and she tried to draw her

hands away to get up but he held onto her. 'I wish there was something I could do or say…'

She shook her head. 'There's nothing anyone can do. For days after Megan died I used to go to her room and just stand by her cot with my eyes closed. I could still smell her, you see…that warm baby smell she had…and pretend that she was there and that it had all been some kind of horrible dream…'

Her voice broke and she heard Nick utter something rough under his breath as he drew her down to enfold her in his strong arms. She wasn't even aware that she was crying at first until she felt the wetness soaking into his pyjama top. She tried to sit up but he held her fast, his cheek pressed against her hair, his hands smoothing her back. It was a while before she realised that he was crying, too, as she felt the dampness in her hair.

'Nick? What is it?' she asked as she drew back to look at him.

'Do you realise that Megan might have been my child if things had worked out all those years ago?' he asked with a catch in his voice.

'Yes,' she whispered softly, because there was no point in denying it.

'I wish—' He broke off abruptly without finishing what he'd been going to say. His voice was raw with emotion as he continued but he avoided her eyes so that she wasn't sure what he was thinking. 'I'm sorry if I awoke a lot of painful memories for you, Abbie.'

She stood up, smoothing her crumpled skirt with hands that weren't quite steady. 'I'm sorry for unburdening them on you like that. I didn't mean to.'

'I'm glad you did.' He smiled tenderly at her. 'It's good to give as well as receive. I hope that telling me about Megan helped in some way.'

'It did.' She realised suddenly that it was true. She rarely spoke about her daughter but it had helped lessen the pain in some strange way, telling Nick about her.

'I'm glad. That's what friends are for, aren't they? To share the good times and the bad.'

'That's right. And as a...friend, Nick, I want you to promise me that you'll try being sensible from now on. David said that you'd brought on this latest attack by doing too much.'

'Probably. I suppose I'll have to accept my limitations, won't I?' He gave her a thin smile which gave little away. 'Anyhow, I'm sorry if I spoiled your evening, Abbie.'

'You didn't. Adam dropped me off early because he's driving up to Edinburgh tomorrow for a conference,' she explained, wanting him to understand the situation, but he merely shrugged.

'I expect he'll soon be in touch. Anyway, thanks again for coming.'

It was a dismissal and she would have needed to be very thick-skinned to have ignored it. She hurried from the room, only pausing long enough to have a word with Nick's parents to reassure them that he was feeling a lot better. How she felt she had no idea, but each time she saw Nick she was left in a state of confusion. He'd been so tender and caring when he'd listened to her pour out her grief over Megan, and then suddenly the barriers had gone up again.

She sighed as she got into her car. He should have a health alert stamped on his forehead stating, WARNING: Too much Nick Delaney is dangerous to your peace of mind!

The trouble was that she wasn't sure she'd take any notice even then!

Abbie called into the surgery mid-morning the next day to pick up some supplies. David was just seeing a patient out and spotted her. 'Oh, I'm glad I've caught you, Abbie. Have you got a minute?'

'Yes, of course.' She followed him into the room and closed the door. 'Problems?'

'Yes and no. First of all, how was Nick when you left him last night?' he asked.

'A lot better. Sounds as though he had a really bad episode that time,' she observed, trying to allow nothing more than professional concern to colour her tone.

'It was. He was in agony when I arrived, and he admitted…reluctantly…that it wasn't the first time he's had severe muscle spasms. He needs regular physiotherapy, preferably on a daily basis, but it's too much to expect him to travel back and forth to the hospital,' David added with a sigh.

'There might be a way round that,' she suggested hesitantly, suddenly recalling the conversation she'd had with Len Parker the previous day. She quickly explained about Mary Parker being a physiotherapist and David nodded.

'Maybe she'd agree to take Nick on as a private patient, you mean? Obviously, I'd need to check out her credentials but that shouldn't be a problem. In fact it might be helpful if we could call on her services for the surgery if she proved suitable. A lot of our patients miss out on physio because of the distances involved in travelling to the hospital,' he said enthusiastically. 'I'll see what the others think, but to my mind it could be the perfect solution all round.'

'I'm sure she'd be glad of the work, too. From what Len said, they're having a tough time of it financially so any extra income would be welcome, I imagine,' she assured him.

'I'll get onto it this afternoon. The other thing was that James asked me to see if you could put Adrian Shaw on your rounds as from tomorrow. He would have spoken to you himself but he's had to go out to an emergency call. Is that OK with you? Say if you're not happy with the idea.'

'No, it's fine. As you know, part of a district nurse's training involves the psychological welfare of patients so I feel quite confident about dealing with Adrian.'

'Good. James had a long talk with Harry and Rose and they admitted that they were worried. It should ease things all round if you supervise Adrian's care,' David said, sounding relieved.

'Maybe I'll pop round there now, just to say hello and let him know I'll be coming to see him,' she suggested.

'Good idea. Thanks, Abbie.'

She drove straight into town and parked in the Fleece's car park. The pub wasn't open yet so she knocked on the house door and Rose let her in. Adrian was in his room so his mother led her upstairs and knocked on the door.

Adrian answered after quite a long interval and Abbie was shocked by how unkempt he looked. He was reluctant to let her into his room but she quietly insisted, while trying to keep things as low-key as possible.

'You remember me, don't you, Adrian? I spoke to you the other day.'

'Yes.' He turned his back on her as he went to the window and pushed back the half-drawn curtains to look out.

'I believe your mother has explained that I'm going to supervise your daily medication, hasn't she?' she continued, looking around. Her eyes alighted on a collection of photographs taped to the dressing-table mirror and she frowned.

Was that Trisha Shepherd in those pictures? It was difficult to tell, with the light being so poor, but when she went to move closer to get a better look, Adrian turned round. He went to the dressing-table and began fiddling with the untidy clutter heaped on top of it, effectively blocking her view of the photographs.

'They're checking up on me, aren't they? They think I don't know that but I do.' He swung round. 'That's why you're here—because they sent you.'

'If you mean the doctors at the surgery then you're right, of course. It's very important that you take your medication, Adrian. You must have been told that before.' Abbie was careful to keep her tone neutral and she saw him shrug.

'Yes.' That was all he said.

'Then I'll see you in the morning. OK?' She gave him a quick smile but he didn't respond. She closed the door and went back downstairs, wondering why she felt so uneasy. Seeing those photographs, it had set off alarm bells but there was no proof that they were of Trisha. They could have been of one of Adrian's friends for all she knew.

She got back in her car and started the engine then came to a sudden decision. She'd call in to have a word with Nick and see what he thought…

And that was the *only* reason she was going to see him? a small voice taunted with just enough scepticism to make her pause. Was she *sure* that wasn't just an excuse?

'Damn, damn, damn!' she said out loud, putting the car into gear with a little more force than was necessary. When had the making of a simple decision become such a battle of wits?

The minute Nick Delaney had become involved. The answer shot back immediately. And a fat lot of comfort it was, too!

CHAPTER EIGHT

IT WAS a few days later when Abbie bumped—quite literally—into Nick. She was leaving the Fleece after her daily visit to see Adrian and was so deep in thought that she didn't notice the wheelchair coming along the pavement.

'Careful!' His hastily shouted warning saved her from a collision, although it scared the life out of her as well.

'Oh!' She pressed a hand to her thundering heart. 'I didn't see you there...sorry.'

'That's OK. Are you sure you're all right, though?' he asked in concern as he saw how white she'd gone.

'Fine, although it's probably taken years off my life!' she replied, summoning a laugh while she tried to steady her racing heart. It wasn't only the shock of the near collision but the unexpected encounter which was making it pound so frantically!

'I hope not,' Nick replied, his tone adding just a fraction more to the statement than maybe it should have done.

'What are you doing in town at this time of the morning, anyway?' she asked quickly, trying to keep her thoughts strictly on track. It wasn't easy because just the sight of him was creating all sorts of emotional havoc.

He looked so much better than the last time she'd seen him for starters—his face was far less strained and his deep blue eyes were unshadowed by pain. He was wearing jeans and a cream polo-necked jumper under a heavy navy peacoat, which emphasised the width of his shoulders. If it hadn't been for the wheelchair, it would have been easy to think there was nothing wrong with him because he looked so healthy and overpoweringly male.

Her pulse skipped a beat as she realised once again how handsome he was. It was an effort to concentrate when he answered her question.

'I had some letters to post so I thought I'd make the trip to the post office before too many people were about,' he explained with a grimace. 'I still can't get used to being the object of so much attention.'

'I imagine most people are interested to know how you're getting on, Nick. They care when something like this happens to one of their own,' she said softly, struggling to get a grip on herself.

'You're probably right. I suppose I'm just hyper-sensitive and hate the idea of becoming some sort of freak show. Anyway, what are you up to? You looked very deep in thought just now. Problems?'

She sighed as she glanced back at the pub. 'I've been to see Adrian.'

'I see. And how are things going?' Nick asked with obvious interest.

'Well…' She hesitated but she had to admit that she'd welcome some expert advice. She was becoming increasingly uneasy about Adrian, although—on the surface at least—things seemed to be going smoothly enough. 'Look, have you got a few minutes to spare? I could do with having a chat with you. I'm rather worried about him but I don't know if I'm not simply looking for problems that aren't really there.'

'Of course. Look, I'll just take these to the postbox and meet you back here at the car.' He gave her a grin which lit up his face. 'Then I'm completely at your disposal, Nurse Fraser!'

'Thanks. I…I was just popping over the road to buy some sandwiches,' she explained hurriedly. When Nick looked at her like that it was easy to believe that he felt something for her, but it would be a mistake to imagine it was anything more than friendship. 'I won't be long but I've a really hectic day today and I won't have time to stop for lunch.'

'How about getting some for me? I could come with you—that's if you can put up with my company, of course.' He shrugged. 'It would give us time to talk about Adrian and give me a change of scene as well. I could do with getting out and about for a while.'

'I... Yes, of course,' she said, taking a deep breath, but the sudden breathlessness wouldn't go away. The thought of spending the day with Nick was something she hadn't planned on and she wasn't sure how she felt about it. It was an effort to keep her tone as casual as his had been. 'What do you fancy, then—ham, cheese, beef? They do a really good selection,' she added, like the perfect hostess.

His eyes glimmered with amusement, giving her the distinct impression that he'd guessed how nervous she was. 'Oh, I'll leave it up to you. The only thing I really loathe is tuna and mayonnaise. Apart from that, I'm not really difficult to please.'

'Right. I'll see you back here, then.' Abbie turned and hurried across the road, already regretting having agreed to his suggestion. Was it really wise to commit herself to a day of his company when just a few minutes caused such turmoil?

She worried about it all the time the sandwiches were being made and wrapped up. She bought cans of Coke as well, and some fruit, then added a box of cakes for good measure and carted the whole lot back to the car. Nick was already there and he whistled when he saw the bulging carrier bag she was toting.

'A veritable picnic, from the look of it. I'm glad I wheedled myself an invitation.'

Abbie laughed, her unease lifting as she heard the questioning note in his voice. Had Nick been wondering if he'd forced her hand and maybe regretted asking to go along? She wasn't sure but it helped take the edge off her nervousness to know that he wasn't as confident as he appeared.

'I'm glad to have the company,' she assured him, and suddenly knew that it was true. 'Now, let's get you sorted and we'll be on our way.'

Once he was safely in the passenger seat, with the wheelchair stowed in the boot, they set off. Abbie drove straight out of town, taking the back road which eventually led to the neighbouring town of Newthwaite.

'Where are we going first?' Nick asked, resting his head comfortably against the back of the seat. It was a sunny day and the pale rays filtering through the windscreen made the strands of silver in his hair shimmer. They caught her attention so that she found her gaze drawn to him while she took stock of the high cheek-bones and strong jaw, those sensuously chiselled lips...

'Boundary Farm.' She fixed her attention on the road, determined to start as she meant to go on. It would be a very stressful day indeed if she allowed her mind to start wandering along those paths. 'Fred Murray had a prostatectomy a few weeks ago. Fortunately, there was no sign of malignancy but he was quite ill after the anaesthetic so they kept him in. I'm going there to check how he's doing and make sure that the wound is healing well.'

'I see. You deal with such a wide variety of work, don't you, Abbie?'

'I do, indeed. District nurses are the medical jacks of all trades! Still, I enjoy the challenge. You never know from one week to the next what you're going to be called on to deal with, and that's part of the fun.'

'I can imagine!' He laughed softly as he glanced at her. 'From post-hospital care to dealing with someone like Adrian Shaw. I'm impressed, Abbie, very impressed.'

There was no denying the sincerity in that statement and she felt a small rush of pleasure. She gave him a quick smile in return. 'Coming from you, Nick, that is praise indeed. I know just how far you've gone in your own field.'

'Yes.' His smile looked a little strained now. 'Although whether I'll ever go back to it remains to be seen. Anyway, what about Adrian? You said that you were worried about him.'

He deliberately denied her the opportunity to say something encouraging and she took the hint. Hopefully, Nick would realise that he still had a lot to offer professionally but he had to make that decision himself. She tried to empty her mind of everything but what had happened in the past few days, wanting to give him a clear picture.

'Well, as you know, I've been going to see Adrian on a daily basis to make sure that he takes his medication,' she explained carefully. 'And to all intents and purposes it has been going quite smoothly. Adrian isn't exactly friendly but he hasn't refused to take the tablets.'

'So, what's the problem, then? I can tell that you're worried.' He turned to look at her, a slight frown drawing his brows together.

'I can't put my finger on it—that's the trouble.' She sighed as she turned onto a narrow back road, which was a short cut to the farm. 'I know he's taking the pills because I see him doing so each morning and yet his behaviour is odd.'

'In what way?' he prompted.

'Well, he's increasingly…"detached" is the only word I can think of. He's there in the room but not there, if you know what I mean. When I speak to him I get the impression that he's listening to something else which I can't hear. Then there's this odd routine we go through each day.'

'What kind of routine?' he asked immediately.

'It's like a set pattern almost. Adrian is always in his

bedroom and I have to go upstairs and knock on his door. He waits until I've knocked five times before he lets me in. Then he does exactly the same thing each day. He walks to the window, draws the curtain backwards and forwards three times in a row, then comes back to me and holds out his hand for the pills.' She laughed uncomfortably.

'It sounds so daft when you put it into words, which is why I haven't spoken to James about it. Am I reading too much into it, Nick, because I'm overly sensitive to the situation?'

'I don't think so. In fact, I'm sure you aren't. Ritualistic behaviour of this kind is a symptom of schizophrenia. I've read Adrian's case notes and there's evidence of it having happened before,' he replied gravely.

'But surely the medication should be controlling his illness?' she protested, turning into the farm road and slowing down to avoid the ruts left by the constant traffic of tractors. 'That's what I can't understand.'

'Are you absolutely certain that Adrian is taking the tablets?' he asked quietly.

'Of course—' she began, then stopped abruptly. 'You think he could be *faking* swallowing them?'

'I think it's very likely. Schizophrenics are very adept at deception. Adrian could be pretending to take his medication, then spitting it out later,' he explained quietly.

'But surely he realises it's in his best interest to take it?' she countered.

'Not if he's ill. Reality will have become blurred in his mind so that he's unable to rationalise any longer.' He shrugged. 'He could genuinely believe that you're trying to poison him, for instance.'

'Then it's worse than I thought!' she exclaimed, drawing up outside the farmhouse and switching off the engine. 'What should I do, Nick? Frankly, I'm at a loss to know how best to handle this.'

'Did James contact the boy's own psychiatrist?' he asked calmly.

'Yes, but he's away for a month. James was given a contact number to call in case of emergencies, but does this constitute an emergency?'

'Certainly there are no grounds for having Adrian sectioned under the Mental Health Act as he isn't endangering himself or anyone else at present. However, it would seem advisable that he be assessed on a voluntary basis,' he explained in that same calm manner, which somehow managed to make the situation so much easier to deal with.

'Then I'll get James to see what can be arranged. Thanks, Nick. It's good to have someone to talk this over with,' she said gratefully.

'You're welcome. And I won't even charge you my usual fee,' he teased.

'Thank heaven for that!' She laughed, leaning over to lift her case from the back seat. 'Right, I'll just go and take a look at Fred. Will you be OK out here?'

'I'll be fine.' He shot a wry look at the uneven ground. 'I'm not experienced enough to try getting my chair over this sort of terrain. Slalom is part of the advanced course!'

Abbie laughed. 'You'll have to start practising.' She got out of the car and hurried to the house to knock on the door. She glanced back as it opened and felt her heart lift as Nick gave her a wave. It was almost like old times, she thought, following Fred inside, she and Nick being able to discuss things…

She sighed as she realised how foolish that was. Those old times were well and truly gone and she'd be setting herself up for a great deal of heartache if she started hankering after them.

*   *   *

'Well, Fred, I must say that I'm pleased with your progress. Your blood pressure is fine and you haven't had any more of those dizzy spells, have you?'

Fred Murray shook his head. He was a down-to-earth man in his late sixties who'd worked hard all his life, running the farm. He'd retired a couple of years previously, relinquishing control to his son, Peter, although he still helped out around the place. 'No, I feel much better, and that's a fact. I can't get over how that anaesthetic knocked me for six. But, then, I've never had an operation before.'

'Well, the wound has healed nicely now. And I imagine you're feeling a lot more comfortable when you pass—'

'Aye, that I do.' Fred hurriedly cut her off and Abbie tried not to smile. A lot of the older men were uncomfortable talking about an operation like this even with a trained nurse. In Fred's view it simply wasn't done to talk about such personal matters with a woman!

'Well, that's good. Anyway, I shall be signing you off today as you don't need any more visits. How's that great-grandson of yours doing, by the way? Have you seen him yet?' she asked, diplomatically changing the subject, to Fred's obvious relief.

'Went to see him yesterday. Real bonny little lad he is, too. Spitting imagine of our Billy when he was born,' Fred told her proudly.

'And have your Peter and Iris come round now the baby's arrived?' Abbie asked, packing everything away. Billy's parents had been horrified when they'd found out that Sophie Jackson was expecting his child, their first grandchild. It was understandable because Billy and Sophie were only teenagers but it hadn't helped an already difficult situation. Thankfully, Sophie's parents had stood by her, and Billy himself was doing all he could to act responsibly.

'No. To hear them talk you'd think it were the first babe ever born out of wedlock!' Fred sighed. 'I've told them they're the ones who'll miss out in the end 'cos it's their grandchild, but they won't listen to sense. Say they won't have anything to do with the little lad.'

'What a shame,' she agreed sadly. 'Let's hope they come round in time.'

Fred saw her out to the car, stopping to have a word with Nick when he spotted him. 'Sorry to hear about your accident, son,' he said bluntly. 'Still, it's good to see that you aren't letting it get you down.' He looked at Abbie and winked. 'Especially not when you've a lovely lass like this to look after you.'

Abbie hastily started the engine, her face flaming with embarrassment. She didn't dare look at Nick to see what he was thinking. She quickly said goodbye and drove away from the farm, aware of the silence which had fallen. She was just trying to think of something to say when Nick spoke.

'That's what people will always think when they see me with a woman—that I'm lucky to have someone to look after me.'

There was such bitterness in his voice that tears stung her eyes. She pulled into the side of the road and turned to him. 'Of course they won't, Nick! Don't be silly.'

'No?' He gave her a thin smile, not trying to hide his disbelief. 'Come on, Abbie, what would any right-minded woman want with me? What could I give her?'

'You! That's what you could give her—you, yourself, the person you are!' She was unaware of the vehemence in her voice as she struggled to convince him. 'You're still the same man you were, Nick. Just because you can no longer walk, that hasn't changed.'

'The same man who can no longer do any of the things he used to do.' He caught hold of her chin, staring deep into her eyes. 'I couldn't protect her if she needed protecting, I couldn't go to her if she were hurt and needed help,

I couldn't even take her in my arms and make love to her. What kind of man is that, Abbie? You tell me!'

The anguish on his face was more than she could bear. 'Don't! Please, don't, Nick. You're torturing yourself unnecessarily.'

She took a quick breath, wondering how to convince him. Obviously, he'd been thinking of his fiancée when he'd said those things, and it hurt to see the damage his broken engagement had done to his self-esteem. In her heart she knew that her opinion didn't really matter and that the only person who could convince him of his own worth was the woman he loved. But she had to try. She couldn't bear to watch him torturing himself this way.

'One day you'll meet someone else and fall in love. It won't make any difference to her whether or not you can walk or…or anything else.'

'No?' He smiled but there was scepticism in the twist of his lips. 'I gave up believing in fairy stories years ago. No sensible woman is going to want to take such a risk.'

'It isn't a fairy story! I—' She stopped abruptly, realising what she'd been about to say—that she'd take that risk, willingly!

'Oh, Abbie, if only—' He broke off as well, his fingers gripping her chin for a moment before he let her go. 'Obviously, we aren't going to agree on this so let's call it quits and not spoil the rest of the day. Where to now?'

She started the car again with hands that shook. What had he been going to say? That if only things had been different, there might have been a chance for them? But what sense was there in even thinking that? If Nick hadn't had the accident they'd never have met again and he'd still be planning to marry Jill…

'Don't, Abbie. There's no point churning it all over. It won't change things.' He shrugged. 'You'll have to forgive me if I get maudlin at times. I've been allowed to become very self-indulgent lately. I shall rely on you to kick me out of my bad habits…as you used to do so effectively in the past.'

He was making a determined effort to lighten the mood and she tried her best to respond. It was better than dwelling on such painful thoughts. 'Now, what bad habits can you possibly be referring to? Always having to win when we played any games? Or always having to be the one to decide what we'd play in the first place? You had so many *bad* habits that it's hard to decide which was worst!'

'Oh, that was below the belt. What about the way you used to sulk if you lost?' he taunted, grinning at her.

'Sulk? Me?' she shot back. 'Come on, Nick, you know that's a complete and utter fabrication!'

'Fabrication? Is that a fancy word for a lie?' he quipped. 'Are you accusing *me* of telling an untruth, Nurse Fraser?'

'If the cap fits…' she retorted. She slowed as they came to the junction, shooting a mocking glance at him.

'Rubbish,' he snorted, glaring at her. 'And it wasn't just sulking you got up to either. How about when I won all your marbles off you that time and you cried your eyes out? Mother made me give them all back even though I'd won them fairly and squarely!'

'Well, you were a better player than me so it wasn't really fair,' she replied, setting off once again.

'So now you're claiming that it was a set-up? That I was some sort of…of junior marble shark?' he demanded.

She couldn't help laughing at the indignation in his voice. 'As I said, Nick, if the cap fits!'

He laughed deeply, his blue eyes crinkling attractively at the corners. 'I never could win when it came down to a war of words. You were always able to tie me in knots, Abbie. Any hint that I'd upset you and I was like putty in your hands.'

'I thought you just said that it was your mother who made you give back those marbles,' she countered.

'I did. But I'd already decided to do so before she spoke to me.' His voice softened, becoming pensive all of a sudden. 'I never could bear to hurt you. That was the trouble.'

It was on the tip of her tongue to remind him how he'd hurt her when he'd stopped coming home and then stopped writing, but she managed to stop herself in time. It would serve no purpose, bringing it up now. It was far better to think about the friendship they'd shared as children than what had happened when they'd got older.

They couldn't change things, and Nick wouldn't want to. He'd eventually met the woman he wanted to marry and, even if it hadn't worked out, there was no pretending that it hadn't happened.

'I'd say that you're suffering from an attack of rose-tinted-spectacle syndrome,' she said quickly, to hide the pain she felt at that thought. 'I believe it often occurs with age.'

'Age! Are you suggesting I'm getting old, Abbie Fraser?' he retorted immediately. He turned to glare at her, picking up on the taunt as she'd intended, and yet there was something in his eyes which made her wonder if he wasn't just playing the game as she was because it was safer...

'You said it, Nick. I didn't.' She shrugged away the uncertainty and was glad that she had when he laughed with what sounded like genuine amusement.

'Well, I could remind you that you're only a year younger than me but that would be such an ungentlemanly thing to do, wouldn't it?' He held his hands up, palms towards her. 'Pax. You win. I concede defeat.'

'Good.' It was an effort to keep up the banter but she refused to let him see how she really felt. 'Now that's sorted out I'd better concentrate on getting some work done. Next stop is Yewthwaite Farm to see Len Parker. OK?'

'Fine by me.' He sat comfortably back in the seat again, seemingly as relaxed as ever so that she was glad she'd managed to avoid any reference to that painful episode in their past. 'Mary Parker has been coming over to give me physio each evening, and it's really helped.'

'I'm glad. I thought of her immediately when David mentioned that you'd benefit from daily sessions. I'm glad it's working out,' she replied softly.

'It is. The muscle spasms are easing off, thanks to the workout she gives me. And I've been swimming most days in the pool so that's helped as well,' he explained.

'Good. A step in the right direction, Nick, isn't it?'

'Maybe.' He shrugged lightly. 'We'll just have to wait and see, won't we?'

It was the first half-positive thing he'd said and her heart lifted. If only Nick would start looking ahead, he'd feel so much better. Once he realised that there was nothing to stop him leading a full life again then maybe he'd return to work...

Her heart sank as it hit her that that would mean him leaving Yewdale. Suddenly she knew that she was going to miss him unbearably when he left. She'd lost Nick once and to lose him a second time was going to be even harder.

CHAPTER NINE

'How about stopping here while we have something to eat?'

Abbie slowed the car as they came to the edge of a small wood. There was a parking area laid out in front of it and half a dozen picnic benches tucked in amongst the trees. On the far side of the wood the land fell away to the valley and the view over Yewdale Water was spectacular enough to attract many tourists. However, apart from a minibus pulled into one side of the parking area, there was no sign of any visitors that day.

'Fine by me. I could do with something to eat. I'm starving,' Nick agreed at once, looking longingly at the carrier bag on the back seat.

'Then we'd better stop. We don't want you passing out with malnutrition, do we?' Abbie laughed as she turned off the road and parked beside the van. 'Do you fancy getting out? It's quite warm today and we could sit at one of those tables.'

'Yes, great. A breath of fresh air would be nice. It's ages since I was here last,' he replied, opening the car door while she lifted the chair from the boot. 'Thanks.'

He quickly swung himself out of the car seat and headed towards the nearest bench, leaving her to follow with their makeshift picnic. His brows rose as she unpacked the bag and spread its contents on the table. 'My, my, you did splash out! Ham *and* beef sandwiches—and what's in here?' He lifted the box lid and peered at the assortment of cakes it contained, grinning wickedly at her. 'I bag that cream bun!'

'Typical! I might have known you'd choose that,' she retorted, sliding a can of cola towards him. 'Anyway, it's probably better that you eat it rather than me. It would only ruin my diet.'

'What diet?' he replied immediately, pushing himself away from the table so that he could treat her to a long, thorough scrutiny. 'You most certainly don't need to be dieting, Abbie, with a figure like that!'

'Flattery will get you an extra cake!' she replied, trying to quell the rush of pleasure she felt at the compliment. Nick was only being kind and didn't mean anything by it, she told herself. But it was hard to ignore the appreciation she'd seen in his eyes.

They ate in contented silence, making short work of the sandwiches and fruit. Nick opened the cake box and took out the cream bun. 'Sure you don't want it? It's your last chance now.' He waved it temptingly under her nose and she laughed.

'No, you can't tempt me, you pest! Anyway, I'm full, really.'

She turned round, resting back on her elbows as she tilted her face up to the sun. It was really warm in the shelter of the trees so that it felt more like summer than autumn, sitting there. She closed her eyes, enjoying the warmth on her face.

'Well, I don't need telling twice, that's for sure.' He ate the cake with obvious enjoyment then wiped his fingers on a napkin and sighed. 'I can't remember the last time I did anything like this. It must be years.'

'Not the sort of sophisticated pastime a man of your standing usually goes in for?' she teased, looking at him through slitted lids.

He tossed the napkin at her, laughing ruefully as she ducked out of the way. 'Cheek! Are you implying that I'm too *stuffy* to enjoy a picnic?'

'Well, you said it, I didn't!' she retorted, getting up to pick up the paper and drop it into the bag with the rest of their rubbish. She sat down again and smiled at him. 'So, what do you usually do for pleasure, Nick, if picnicking isn't on the agenda?'

'Oh, nothing very exciting.' He shrugged. 'Occasional visits to the theatre, a few dinner parties, although they're usually more for business than pleasure. To be honest, I've been so wrapped up in my work in the past few years that I haven't spent all that much time just enjoying myself.'

'What a shame. And was your fiancée happy with the situation?' she asked before she thought better of it. She coloured as he looked at her, and quickly began clearing up the remains of their meal. 'Sorry, it isn't any of my business…'

'Hey, you're allowed to ask questions.' He took the bag from her and neatly stored the Cellophane wrappings off their sandwiches inside. 'Jill was as involved in her work as I was in mine. She's very ambitious and devotes most of her time and energy to her career.' He shrugged lightly. 'Ours was never the sort of relationship whereby we spent all our free time together.'

'I expect that would have changed once you were married,' Abbie said quietly, wondering why she felt driven to continue when it caused her such pain. The thought of Nick and this woman once planning a future together was difficult to come to terms with.

'I doubt it. Jill made it plain that she didn't want a family so I imagine we'd have carried on much the same way as we were,' he stated calmly.

'But would you have been happy with that, Nick?' she asked, shocked by his seemingly easy acceptance of the situation.

'It didn't worry me, if you want the truth.' He looked at her and his expression was suddenly hard to decipher. 'I haven't given much thought to the possibility of having children in recent years. And now there seems even less reason to think about it.'

She felt an immediate pang as she realised how the question must have hurt him in the circumstances. Yet, short of apologising, there was nothing she could say, and she sensed that would just make matters worse. Nick didn't need reminding that he might not be able to father a child. The thought caused her such intense pain that she quickly got to her feet in case he realised that something was wrong. Yet why should it upset her so much that Nick might never be able to have children? She wasn't sure.

'Well, I suppose we'd better be going…' she began, then stopped as she heard voices. She'd just turned to see who was coming when a group of children appeared from the trees.

'Abbie!'

One of the children came running over to her and she smiled as she realised that it was Emily, David's youngest child. 'Hello, Emily. What are you up to?'

'Miss Wilson brought us here so we could collect leaves for the nature table,' Emily informed her excitedly. She held out a huge handful of fallen leaves for Abbie's inspection. 'See, this is from an oak tree and this is from an ash and this—'

'Now, Emily, don't go pestering Nurse Fraser,' Ruth Wilson, the class teacher, chided, coming over to join them. 'I'm sorry about this. I bet you were just enjoying the peace and quiet when we had to come along and spoil it!'

Abbie laughed. 'Oh, don't worry about it! We were just about to leave anyway. Have you met Nick Delaney, by the way, Ruth?'

'Not till now. Pleased to meet you, Mr Delaney.' Ruth offered her hand and Nick shook it.

'Make that Nick, please,' he said with a smile that

brought a touch of colour to the other woman's face. It was obvious that Ruth found him attractive and no wonder, Abbie thought, trying to ignore the small spurt of jealousy she felt. Nick was a very attractive man.

'Nick, then.' Ruth treated him to an even warmer smile then started to gather the children together. Within minutes they were lined up beside the minibus while she counted heads. 'That's fourteen so we're one short. Now, who's missing…? Oh, I might have known! Has anyone seen Darren Jackson?' she asked wearily.

'He was behind us in the woods,' Emily said helpfully. 'Close to where we found that badger's sett.'

Ruth looked worried. 'And you didn't see him after that, Emily?'

'No, Miss Wilson. Shall I go and find him?' Emily offered immediately.

'No, no, I don't want you getting lost as well,' Ruth declared hurriedly. A couple of the children's mothers had come along on the trip to help and she had a word with them then turned to Abbie with a grimace. 'I'd better go and track young Darren down. That child has a positive talent for getting up to mischief.'

'It runs in the family,' Abbie replied with a knowing laugh. 'The Jackson children are always in the thick of things.'

'Don't I know it? Each one of the three boys has been in my class, worse luck,' Ruth replied wryly, before hurrying off to find the missing child. The other children were soon running about, giving the two mums a hard time as they tried to keep order. Abbie grimaced as the noise level rose a good few decibels.

'So much for enjoying the peace,' she said to Nick with a rueful laugh.

He smiled as he watched the children racing around. 'They're having fun, though. I bet these kids will think back to this day in a few years' time, and it will be one of those wonderful memories they never forget.'

'Mmm, I expect you're right.' She frowned as she tied a knot in the top of the carrier bag to stop the litter spilling out. 'What's your favourite memory from when you were a child?'

'Oh, that day we went off on a hike to Newthwaite,' he said immediately. 'We must have been about eleven or twelve at the time and your mother packed us a picnic— do you remember?'

'Yes,' she replied quietly. 'We walked for miles, or what seemed like miles at the time. Then we stopped by the stream to eat our lunch and went paddling and—'

'And you fell in the water and got soaked,' he finished for her. He smiled at her with such tenderness that a lump came to her throat. 'I remember giving you my sweater to wear while I raced around, waving your dress in the air to dry it off. We must have looked like a couple of tramps when we got back home.'

'I expect we did,' she said, touched that he remembered the day in such detail. She'd never imagined that he'd set such store by the things they'd done together as children.

'How about you, Abbie? What's your fondest memory of when you were a kid?' he asked softly.

'I don't know...' She shrugged. 'There were so many good times, weren't there? Snowball fights in your garden at Christmas, pond-dipping in the spring for frog spawn... Oh, do you remember us bringing home that huge frog we found?'

'Do I?' He grimaced. 'The wretched thing escaped and got into the kitchen—'

'And my mother found it sitting on a shelf in the larder and nearly screamed the house down,' she finished for him.

'Father threatened to make me stay at school for the whole of the summer holidays if I ever did anything like that again. I had to apologise to your mother *and* scrub the larder out. It took me a whole day to do it, too!'

'Really? I don't remember that. Why didn't I have to help you?' she asked with a frown.

'Oh, I told my parents that it was my fault and that you didn't know I'd brought the frog back with me.' He laughed lightly. 'There was no point in you getting into trouble as well as me, Abbie.'

The lump in her throat seemed to get bigger. 'You were always taking the blame for me, Nick. Any time you thought I'd get into trouble for some prank or other, you said it was your fault.'

'Well, I was older than you...as you pointed out before,' he replied tartly. 'Now, shall I take that bag over to the litter bin and dump it?'

He lifted the carrier from the table and wheeled himself over to the bin. Nick had gone out of his way to take care of her when they were children and, remembering that now, it awoke all sorts of feelings inside her, the strongest of which was a simple desire that they could go back to those days.

He turned round and her heart ached as she realised how futile it was to wish for such a thing. There had been too many changes to both their lives in the intervening years.

Nick had just got into the car when Ruth came back with young Darren. The boy was carrying something in his arms and Abbie frowned as she saw the other children cluster around him. 'I wonder what's going on?' she murmured as the whole group came rushing towards them.

'Darren's found a rabbit and it's hurt its leg,' Emily said, racing on ahead. 'Can you make it better, Abbie...please?'

'I don't know, love. Let me see.' Her heart sank as Darren held the terrified creature towards her and she saw the gash down its hind leg. It was so deep that she could see the bone. 'What do you think, Nick?' she asked quietly, turning to him in concern.

'It doesn't look too good,' he said just as softly, conscious of the children who were listening anxiously to every word.

'You can do something for it, though, can't you? You're a nurse and you're supposed to be able to make things better!' Darren's tone was belligerent but Abbie could see tears in his eyes as he looked down at the shivering little animal.

'I don't know, Darren. It seems to be very badly hurt,' she explained gently, wondering what to do for the best. Several of the children looked really upset and one little girl had started to cry.

'I think the best thing would be if we took it to the vet,' Nick put in, quietly taking charge. He turned to the children, deliberately distracting their attention by giving them something to do. 'We're going to need a box to carry the rabbit in and some nice dry leaves to make it a comfortable bed.'

'There's a cardboard box in the back of the bus which had our drinks in it,' Emily announced, rushing off to fetch it.

'And the children can collect some dry leaves. There are plenty just beneath the trees over there,' Ruth instructed, taking her lead from him as she sent the children off to collect them. She turned to them once they were out of earshot. 'I'm really sorry to put you on the spot like this. I know there probably isn't much you can do for the poor little thing. The children were so upset when they saw it, you see, and then Emily said that you'd be able to do something…'

'Don't worry about it, Ruth,' Abbie assured her. 'Nick and I will drop the rabbit off at the vet's on our way.'

'Well, if you're sure?' Ruth sounded relieved.

Obviously, the thought of having to drive back to town with a bus full of distressed children wasn't something she'd been looking forward to.

When Emily arrived back with the cardboard box Abbie helped her punch air holes into its sides and lid then let the children line it with leaves. Darren carefully placed the terrified rabbit inside and closed the lid.

'He'll be all right, won't he?' he asked, running a grimy hand over his eyes and trying to pretend that he wasn't crying.

'We'll make sure that the vet takes good care of him,' Nick assured him, being careful not to make any promises. 'Now if you give me the box I'll hold it so that he doesn't get jolted around too much.'

The whole group waved them off as Abbie backed the car onto the road. She headed back the way they'd come, taking the road to Newthwaite where there was a veterinary surgery. Fortunately it was open when they got there so she quickly parked outside and took the box from Nick.

'Ask him to do whatever he can and send the bill to me, will you, Abbie?' he said.

'I will. Thanks, Nick. It's good of you to offer,' she said softly, before hurrying across the pavement. Not many people would care what happened to a wild rabbit but it was so typical of him. Nick had always cared, whether it was about animals or people. It was an intrinsic part of his character, what made him the person he was—kind, compassionate, generous, loving…

She took a deep breath as she pushed open the surgery door. There were so many different ways of loving, though, and maybe Nick still loved her in a way. Certainly, everything he'd said that day pointed to the fact that he still felt affection for her. But in her heart she knew that it wasn't enough. She didn't want him just to love her as a friend but as a woman. The fact that it would never happen didn't make her want it any less.

It was late by the time Abbie got back to the surgery. She'd dropped Nick off at home earlier in the afternoon then had carried on with her calls. They'd both been rather quiet on the drive back from Newthwaite. She'd had her own thoughts to contend with but Nick had appeared equally distracted, although his silence could have been put down to tiredness. She only hoped that he hadn't done too much and ruined all the physiotherapist's hard work.

'Oh, I was hoping you'd call in. How are you fixed for tonight?'

She'd just finished sorting her case notes for filing when Elizabeth collared her. 'Depends what you want me for,' she replied cagily.

'Nothing awful,' her friend retorted with a grin. 'The famous shoes have arrived so I thought I'd bring them round tonight to see how they go with your dress. I'm hoping that the dye matches this time,' she added pithily.

Abbie laughed. She was to be chief bridesmaid at Elizabeth's and James's wedding in December. The arrangements had been made for some time now but efforts to get her shoes dyed the same colour as her dress had proved extremely difficult. 'They can't be any worse, surely? The last pair were green rather than lavender!'

'I know. Can you just imagine what they'd have looked like?' Elizabeth grimaced. 'Anyway, is it all right if I pop round at about eight o'clock? You aren't going out?'

Abbie's brows rose. 'You make it sound as though I lead a hectic social life and am never at home.'

'Oh, I just thought that you might be going out with Adam,' Elizabeth said airily.

'Why on earth should you think that—?' she began, then groaned. 'What has Laura been telling you?'

'Nothing! Honestly, she hasn't said a thing... Well, she did just happen to mention that he'd taken you out for a drink,' she admitted.

'Did she, indeed?' Abbie sighed. 'I never thought Laura, of all people, would stoop to...to matchmaking!'

'Oh, I'm sure she isn't trying to do that,' Elizabeth said soothingly but without much conviction. 'Anyway, you have to admit that Adam is rather nice.'

Abbie rolled her eyes. 'Now you're at it as well. I don't believe this. Yes, Adam is very nice. And yes again, he did take me for a drink. End of story. It isn't the start of a big romance so don't get your hopes up.'

'OK! OK!' Elizabeth held her hands up. 'I didn't mean to go poking my nose in where it isn't wanted.'

'Oh, I'm sorry, too. I shouldn't have snapped like that. I'm just a bit touchy about the subject of Adam Mackenzie. Even Nick seems to think...' She stopped as she realised how revealing the slip might be.

'Nick thinks that you and Adam are an item?' Elizabeth frowned. 'And is that a problem?'

'No, of course not. He isn't interested in what I do.' She turned away to check the diary, although she'd already noted down what appointments she had the following day.

'But you'd like him to be? I didn't realise, Abbie.'

'I don't know what you mean,' she said quickly. She avoided Elizabeth's eyes as she picked up her case and headed for the door before her friend could say anything more on the subject. 'I'll see you tonight, then. How about if I get a bottle of wine and we have a girls' night in? James is on call tonight, isn't he?'

'Yes, that would be lovely. It's ages since we had a good gossip,' Elizabeth replied lightly, but Abbie wasn't blind to the speculation in her eyes. She hurried from the surgery, wishing she hadn't made that revealing slip. What point was there in wearing her heart on her sleeve? Nick wasn't interested in her that way—end of story. There certainly wasn't going to be a happy-ever-after where they were concerned!

'Not too bad, wouldn't you say? Definitely an improvement on the last pair.'

Abbie stepped in front of the mirror and took another look at the satin slippers, peeping out from under the hem of the dress. It had been Elizabeth's idea that she try it on so that they could see how well the shoes matched. Now she couldn't help feeling rather pleased as she studied her reflection.

The deep lavender silk *was* the perfect foil for her hair, while the slight *décolleté* neckline made the most of her full bust. The dress had a fitted bodice and a full skirt draped over layers of stiffened petticoats, a style which made her waist look far tinier than it really was. All in all, it had to be the most feminine dress she'd ever worn and such a contrast to her usual everyday uniform that she was reluctant to take it off.

'Eat your heart out, Scarlett O'Hara, is all I can say!' Elizabeth replied with a laugh. 'The dress looks great on you, Abbie. And the shoes are perfect this time, thank heavens.'

'Let's hope that was the last hitch, then. From here on in it's going to be plain sailing. I think that sounds like a cue for a toast, don't you? Come on, pass your glass.'

Picking up the bottle of wine from the dressing-table, she refilled both their glasses. 'Here's to the wedding of the year—may it go smoothly from now on!'

'Amen to that!' Elizabeth took a sip of the wine then sighed wistfully as Abbie reluctantly began to take off the dress. 'Sometimes I think it's *never* going to happen. Marrying James is the thing I want most in the whole world and I'm simply counting the days!' She laughed self-consciously. 'I bet that's how every woman feels when she's about to get married, though, isn't it?'

'Probably,' Abbie replied shortly, quickly turning away to put the dress on its hanger. Elizabeth's comment had touched a nerve because she knew deep down that she'd never approached her own marriage in that frame of mind. She'd looked forward to the day but there had been no sense of urgency to be Paul's wife, certainly not how Elizabeth had described it. Was it any wonder that it hadn't worked out?

The thought made her feel just a bit guilty so she quickly shut it from her mind as she carefully stowed the dress in the wardrobe. 'Right, that's that, then. Panic over. The shoes are fine and the dress is gorgeous, although I doubt anyone's going to notice. All eyes will be on you that day, Liz—'

She broke off as the doorbell suddenly rang. 'Now, who can that be?' she demanded, reaching for her robe and quickly pulling it on. She picked up her glass and took a swallow of wine. 'I wasn't expecting anyone. I'll see who it is and get rid of them.'

Still holding the glass, she ran downstairs and opened the door then blinked as she found Nick outside. It was such a shock to see him that she couldn't think of anything to say.

'I'm sorry, I seem to have called at an awkward moment,' he said tersely, putting his own interpretation on her silence. His eyes moved deliberately from the wine glass to skim the length of her body and she was shocked to see the anger they held as they came back to her face.

'Mother asked if I'd bring these round for you. Something to do with the Guides and their first-aid badges. She couldn't come herself as she's had to go out.'

'Thank you.' She accepted the package he offered her,

trying to work out what was wrong. Had she done something to upset him? But what?

'Don't mention it.' He swung the wheelchair round and headed back down the path then paused to glance back. The light for the streetlamp had leached all the colour from his face so that it looked as though it had been carved from stone, and she shivered involuntarily. 'Oh, before I forget, thanks for taking pity on me today. I'm sure entertaining the sick and lonely isn't part of your job description but, then, you always did have a fine sense of duty, Abbie. Anyway, I won't keep you any longer. I'm sure you have better things to do with your night.'

He cast a pointed glance at the lighted bedroom window then wheeled himself away. Abbie watched open-mouthed as he went to his car. He had obviously perfected the technique of getting in and out by himself and had little trouble sliding into the driving seat and only a bit more manoeuvring the chair behind the seat. He didn't look at her again as he started the engine and drove away.

She went back inside and closed the door, still trying to work out what had been wrong with him. He'd seemed perfectly fine when she'd left him that afternoon—a bit subdued, but that was all. What had happened in the intervening hours to prompt that last acerbic comment?

She gasped as it hit her all of a sudden. Her shocked gaze flew from the glass she was holding to the satin robe she was wearing, and she gulped. Add those to the light in the bedroom window and the picture was starting to take on quite a different slant to what it actually portrayed!

Had Nick added everything up and arrived at entirely the wrong conclusion—that there was a man waiting in her bedroom for her to join him for a night of passion? She had the horrible feeling that was the answer!

She took a much-needed sip of wine, trying to work out what she should do about it. Should she ring him up when he got home and explain? Should she go round there and see him? Or should she simply let him go on believing what he wanted to? After all, what real difference could it make to Nick if there *was* a man in her life? That, of course, was the most difficult question of all because she already knew the answer!

CHAPTER TEN

'HE's doing really well, Sophie. He's already regained his birth weight, which is excellent.'

Abbie gently lifted the squirming baby out of the scales and handed him back to his young mother. She'd been visiting Sophie Jackson daily since she'd come home from hospital, and was impressed by how well the teenager was coping with looking after baby William.

'He's been so good,' Sophie said, cuddling the baby to her. 'Of course, my mum's been brilliant, showing me what to do and helping me look after him, but he's such a good baby. He isn't a bit of trouble, taking his feeds.'

'I can tell. Otherwise he wouldn't be gaining weight as fast as he is!' Abbie laughed as she went to take another look at the little boy. 'You're gorgeous, aren't you, poppet? I bet your daddy is really proud of you, too.'

'Oh, Billy's thrilled to bits!' Sophie declared as she carried the baby over to his crib. It was rather cramped in the small room with her bed and William's cot, and the furniture was a bit battered. However, everything was spotlessly clean, from the freshly laundered sheets in William's cot to the pile of baby linen neatly stacked on the old chest of drawers.

It couldn't be easy for the Jackson family, accommodating another child into their household, Abbie thought as she looked around. As well as Sophie and the three boys, there was young Chloe, who'd been so very ill recently when she'd been diagnosed with leukaemia. Although Chloe's illness was in remission, it had been a worrying time for Annie and Barry Jackson and she was full of admiration for the way they'd coped with this most recent crisis.

'I just wish Billy's parents would come round to the idea now that the baby is here,' Sophie said sadly as she fastened the poppers on the baby's lemon sleepsuit. 'They haven't even been to see William yet.'

Abbie sighed, not sure what to say. 'It must be hard for them, love. Not everyone reacts the same way. Billy's parents will accept the idea in time, you'll see. Anyway, how are you feeling in yourself? Those stitches aren't giving you any trouble?'

'No, they're fine. I feel great, in fact. I'm hoping to go back to college in a few weeks' time. I've got an interview next week with the principal and I'm hoping he'll let me start before the end of this term.'

'Why, that's brilliant, Sophie! It's the community college you're going to, isn't it? I believe there's a crèche there so you'll be able to take William with you,' Abbie said enthusiastically.

'That's right. It should work out OK but I'll have to wait and see. Billy's doing all he can to help, working at Mr Shepherd's place to get some extra money to pay for what the baby needs, so I reckon we'll manage somehow,' Sophie said positively.

'I'm sure you will,' Abbie agreed sincerely. 'Right, I'll see you tomorrow, then.'

She made her own way downstairs while Sophie finished dressing the baby. Annie Jackson must have heard her coming down the stairs because she popped her head round the sitting-room door. 'You off now, Abbie?'

'Yes. Everything is fine. I must say that Sophie's managing really well. She was just telling me she's going back to college shortly.'

'That's right. Wants to do her A levels, she does, so as

she can get herself a decent job,' Annie explained, opening the front door.

'Good for her. I'm sure she'll succeed, too. Right, I'd better be off, then…'

'Oh, before I forget, thanks for what you did for our Darren. He was thrilled to bits when he found out that poor little rabbit is going to be all right. Mr Delaney called after school yesterday and took him to the vet's so he could see it. He was full of it last night—talked of nothing else, in fact!'

'I…I'm glad it's getting better,' Abbie said quietly, struggling not to show her disappointment. She quickly said goodbye and got into her car, telling herself that it was silly to feel hurt that Nick hadn't invited her along as well. He'd probably not given her a thought, if truth be told. He certainly hadn't made any attempt to contact her since the night he'd called at her house, which was almost a week ago now!

That thought accompanied her as she drove through the town and pulled up outside the Fleece. It didn't help that she was forced to admit that she might be partly at fault for the lack of contact between her and Nick. She could have phoned him. And said what? That she didn't have a lover keeping her bed warm? Fat lot he'd care!

Harry Shaw answered the door to her knock and she forgot about her own troubles as soon as she saw his face. 'What's wrong?' she asked, quickly stepping inside.

'Adrian's disappeared. He didn't come home last night and Rose and I have no idea where he's got to,' he explained anxiously.

'Have you tried everywhere you can think of where he might be?' she asked, her heart sinking when he nodded.

'Everywhere! The hostel where he stayed once, his former digs, even the hospital. No one has seen hide nor hair of him. We…we don't know what to do for the best,' Harry finished, running a shaking hand over his face. He seemed to have aged a good ten years overnight and her heart went out to him.

'Did Adrian take his tablets with him?' she asked without much hope.

'No. The bottle's still in the cupboard.' He sighed heavily. 'You may as well know the whole story. Adrian hasn't been swallowing the tablets. Rose found a pile of them wrapped up in a tissue under his mattress yesterday. He…he must have been pretending to take them, then spitting them out.'

It was just as Nick had suggested, she realised with a sinking heart. 'Do you know what prompted Adrian to go off like this? Was he upset about anything? Did you have a row, perhaps?'

'It was all because of that letter from the hospital that came yesterday. Dr Sinclair told me that he was going to get onto them because he was concerned. They wrote to Adrian, asking him to go in to see them just to have a chat.'

'And it upset him?' Abbie asked quietly.

'Yes. He got very agitated. Kept pacing up and down, muttering, then shut himself in his room. Rose took him up some dinner but he wouldn't open the door to her.' Harry sighed. 'He must have slipped out while we were busy behind the bar last night. We didn't hear him so there was no way we could have stopped him.'

'You mustn't blame yourself, Harry. None of this is your fault. You've done all you could in the circumstances,' she assured him, but she knew it must be little comfort. Harry must be worried sick about his son and she had to admit that she was deeply concerned herself. Without the benefit of medication, Adrian's illness could easily spiral out of control. She came to a swift decision.

'I need to speak to James about this. Can I use your phone?'

'Of course,' he replied at once, showing her into the back room. 'I'll just go and see how Rose is. I made her stay in bed and rest as she was so upset last night. Why did this all have to happen, eh?'

James sounded as concerned as she was when Abbie explained the situation to him. He decided to get straight on to the hospital where Adrian had been a patient to see what they advised. 'I'm going to give Nick a call as well, and see what he thinks. In fact, is there any chance you could call round and see him, Abbie? I'm up to my eyes in it here this morning, otherwise I wouldn't ask. Elizabeth has had to go out on a call and it's left us short-handed.'

'Of course. I…I'll pop in and have a word with him now, then get back to you,' she agreed, her heart beating painfully fast at the thought of seeing Nick again.

'And, although I hate to do it, I think I'd better have a word with the police.' James's tone was very grave. 'We daren't overlook the fact that Adrian might become a danger to other people as well as himself in his present unbalanced state.'

Abbie quietly agreed, although her heart was heavy as she waited for Harry to come back. She told him what was happening, wishing there was something she could say to help, but there was little anyone could do other than find the boy as soon as possible.

She left the pub, promising to get in touch as soon as she heard anything, and drove straight to the Delaneys' house. Nick's car was parked in the drive, its door standing open as though he was planning on going out. She hesitated when she saw it but the situation was too urgent to warrant a delay.

She got out to knock on the front door but just at that moment Nick himself appeared from the back of the house. Her pulse gave a small leap as she took rapid stock of the well-cut dark suit he was wearing with a pale blue shirt and burgundy silk tie before she suddenly became aware that she was staring.

She looked away at once, trying to confine her thoughts strictly to what she was there for. 'I'm sorry to bother you, Nick. I can see that you're on your way out but we have a bit of a crisis on our hands.'

'Is it Adrian Shaw?' he asked crisply, his tone giving nothing away. If he was pleased to see her, or even annoyed by the delay, he gave little sign, and Abbie felt quite irrationally annoyed. Did he have to make it so obvious that he couldn't care less if he saw her or not?

'Yes. Adrian has gone missing. His parents haven't seen him since yesterday. And, as you suspected, he's only been pretending to take his medication. His mother found a cache of tablets under the mattress.'

'Damn!' Nick sighed heavily as he glanced at the car so that she wasn't sure what he was referring to exactly. 'Look, you'd better come inside so that we can talk this through.'

'I don't want to delay you…' she began.

'It doesn't matter. Anyway, I can hardly grumble about a few minutes' delay after interrupting you the other night.' The smile he gave her was tinged with cynicism. 'Still, I'm sure you didn't let it spoil your evening, Abbie.'

'Oh, it didn't!' Two could play at this game, she decided, disliking both his tone and the assumption he'd made. 'It was a lovely evening. I really enjoyed it.'

'I'm sure you did.' He swung the wheelchair round and led the way into the house via the conservatory, closing the door behind them to keep in the heat. The scent of the orchids was pervasive, filling the moist air with its exotic fragrance. Abbie drew in a deep lungful as she followed Nick to the centre of the room and sat down on a bench, but it didn't do much to soothe her rising temper.

'Right, tell me what happened from the beginning,' he

instructed in that same terse, no-nonsense tone which she disliked so much.

She quickly related everything Harry had told her about the previous day's events, keeping her tone as businesslike as his had been. 'James is getting on to the hospital and he's decided that he'd better contact the police. Do you think that Adrian could constitute a danger to anyone?'

'It's impossible to say without speaking to him. There are no hard and fast rules when dealing with this illness. Each individual case is different. Just because a person is schizophrenic, it doesn't naturally follow that he'll be dangerous. Unfortunately, the media tends to focus on extreme cases where violence has occurred. Many schizophrenics simply become withdrawn and are unable to care for themselves.'

'I see. Adrian hasn't shown any tendency towards being violent in the past so is that a good sign, would you say?' she queried.

'Maybe, but, as I say, there aren't any hard and fast rules. You have to understand that he's probably suffering delusions so that everyday things—no matter how innocuous— could take on a new significance to him,' he explained quietly, trying to put it in terms she could understand. 'He might imagine that they constitute a danger to him and react accordingly. To his mind he is simply protecting himself.'

'So it's very hit and miss, then? There isn't any way we can predict how he'll react?'

'I'm afraid not. All I can say is that it's imperative that he's found and that he receives treatment,' Nick concluded, pushing back his cuff to check his watch.

Abbie took the hint and got quickly to her feet. 'Thank you anyway. I'll tell James what you just told me and we'll go from there. I'm sorry if I've held you up. I hope I haven't made you late.'

'Not at all,' he assured her politely. He sounded like a

stranger when he spoke to her in that stiffly formal manner. It was such a contrast to the way he'd been that day they'd spent together that her heart ached.

She swung round to leave before he saw how much it hurt to have him treat her like that, and in her haste she never saw the coil of hosepipe snaked across the floor. She gave a sharp gasp of shock as her foot snagged in the hose, pitching her off balance. Instinctively, she put out her hands to save herself and cried out as her right wrist twisted painfully as she fell on it.

'Abbie! Are you all right?' He was beside her in a second, his hand firm and strong as he helped her to her feet. He helped her sit back on the bench, positioning the wheelchair as close beside her as he could get it. 'You've hurt your wrist. Let me see.'

His touch was infinitely gentle as he took hold of her arm and examined her wrist. It was already starting to swell and was throbbing painfully. 'It looks as though you've sprained it, although we can't rule out the possibility that it might be broken. You need a cold compress on it right away to reduce the swelling. Come on, let's get it sorted out.'

'It'll be fine, Nick, honestly,' she protested, inwardly wondering how she was going to drive with it in this state. 'You're just on your way out…'

'It isn't fine! Anyone can see that. So stop arguing and do as you're told for once.' His sudden smile took the sting out of the words. 'Trust me, I'm a doctor!'

'And that's supposed to inspire confidence?' she retorted, albeit shakily, and heard him laugh. He led the way through the house to his room, went straight to the bathroom and ran cold water into the low-level sink. Taking a hand towel from the rack, he soaked it in water then wrung it out.

'Come over here while I put this round your wrist,' he instructed.

Abbie did as she was told, pulling over a cork-topped stool to sit on as he draped a dry towel over his knees then gently placed her injured arm on top of it while he examined the swelling once more. 'It's starting to bruise now. You'll definitely need it X-rayed in case it's fractured.'

'I hope it isn't,' she declared. 'I don't know how I'm going to manage if it's put in plaster.'

'Cross that bridge when you come to it. Now, hold still while I put this round it. It should help reduce the swelling and make it more comfortable.' It took only seconds to wrap the cold, wet towel around her wrist. Abbie bit her lip against the pain, although Nick was as gentle as he could be. He frowned when he saw how white she'd gone.

'Does it hurt very much?' he asked gently, his blue eyes full of concern.

'Just a bit,' she whispered, blinking back a few tears, although if she was honest it wasn't just the pain which made her feel weepy. It was having him look at her with such concern after the cold way he'd treated her before. Suddenly she knew that she couldn't bear to let him carry on believing what he did.

'About the other night, Nick, when you came round—'

'Forget it!' he said shortly, reaching over to pull the plug out of the basin so that the water could drain away. 'It hasn't anything to do with me what you do.'

He was so stubborn! So…so pig-headed when he chose to be! Abbie glared at him and saw his brows rise, but suddenly she didn't care what he thought. He was going to hear the truth whether he liked it or not.

'You're right. It isn't any of your business. However, just for the record, it was Elizabeth at my house the other night. I'm going to be a bridesmaid at her wedding and she'd brought some shoes round for me try on with my dress, and that's what we'd been doing when you called.' She gave a harsh little laugh and stood up. 'You didn't catch me *in flagrante delicto*, Nick, if that's what you thought!'

She turned and strode to the door, suddenly wishing that she hadn't said anything. It was obvious from his silence that he couldn't care less...

'Is that the truth, Abbie?'

Maybe she should have been annoyed that he doubted her, but there was something in his voice which made that impossible. She turned to face him again, feeling the shiver that danced down her spine as she saw his expression. She couldn't recall seeing such need on anyone's face before...

He uttered something harsh before he looked away, his head bowed as though he couldn't bear her to see how he felt. 'I'm sorry. Obviously, I jumped to conclusions and I apologise.'

'You did.' She took a deep breath but something was pushing her to ask the question even though she knew it might not be wise. 'Why were you so annoyed when you thought that I might have a...a...' She balked at the words and tailed off uncertainly, flinching as he laughed harshly. When he looked at her there was such bitterness in his eyes that she almost recoiled until it struck her that it wasn't aimed at her but at himself.

'That you might have a man waiting in your bed for you? After all, that *is* what I thought, and is it any wonder?' He took a deep breath and his tone was suddenly flat. 'You're a beautiful woman, Abbie. There must be a lot of men who'd want to spend a night in your arms. I envy them.'

Her eyes burned with tears as she suddenly understood. She swallowed hard but there was a catch in her voice she couldn't hide. 'Do you, Nick?'

'Yes!' His eyes blazed at her for a moment before he looked away again. 'I'm sorry. I have no right to say such a thing. Your personal life isn't any of my business.'

Maybe if she hadn't heard the echo of pain in his voice

she could have continued thinking that he didn't care. But she did hear it and it set loose so many emotions inside her that her head spun until gradually it became clear what she was going to do even though she wasn't sure it was sensible.

'Maybe it isn't as impossible as you think, Nick,' she said softly. 'There's an easy way to find out.'

His eyes darkened as he immediately understood what she meant yet she was unprepared for his anger. 'Damn you, Abbie! Do you have any idea how that makes me feel? Do you really think I want your…your *charity*?'

His tone was fierce enough to make her flinch but something gave her the strength to look behind the harsh words to what had prompted them. And she knew in her heart that it was fear that made him reject her, nothing else.

She went and knelt in front of him, making it impossible for him to turn away. 'Who said anything about charity, Nick? I didn't.'

'Abbie…' He tried to speak then broke off as though he couldn't find the words he wanted. Reaching out, he cupped her cheek and she could feel his hand trembling. 'It would be a crazy thing to do. Can't you see that for yourself?' he murmured, yet even as he spoke he was drawing her towards him.

Abbie closed her eyes as his mouth found hers so gently that it felt as though she were dreaming what was happening. There was just the soft brush of his lips against hers, a momentary feeling of warmth which ran through her like wine, and then he was drawing away…

She gave a small cry of protest, unaware that she'd made any sound at all until she felt him still. Just his fingertips were touching her now and her heart quailed at the thought of losing this last fragile link.

She laid her hand over his, pressing his palm against her cheek, hearing the softly uttered protest he made. She was

so afraid that he'd snatch his hand away that a tear slid
down her cheek and was quickly followed by another until
she was crying in earnest.

'Don't…please, don't, Abbie. I can't bear it!'

The hoarseness of his deep voice seemed to rasp against
every nerve in her body so that she shuddered convulsively
and heard him groan. When his fingers slid into her hair as
he drew her towards him once more she waited for the
touch of his mouth with every part of her that was alive
and feeling, but even then she wasn't prepared for the turmoil it unleashed as his lips found hers.

This kiss was very different from the one before because
there was no hesitancy now, little delicacy, and yet it was
just as wonderful in a rawly unbridled way.

Nick held nothing back as he kissed her with every scrap
of pent-up emotion he felt so that she was assaulted by the
rawness of his hunger, by the ferocity of his need, by his
overwhelming desire to be, for this moment, just a man
kissing the woman he wanted to make love to!

He drew back at last, resting his forehead against hers
as a shudder worked its way through his body. 'You almost
make me forget, Abbie.'

She cradled his cheek in her hand, 'It could happen,
Nick. After all, there was that time in the pool—'

He kissed her quickly, stopping the words on her lips as
though he was afraid to hear them. 'That doesn't mean I'm
capable of making love to you. You know that as well as
I do.'

'Do you want to?' she asked softly, wondering how it
was possible to speak so calmly when her mind was in
turmoil.

'Yes! No! Hell, I don't know what I want!' He framed
her face between his hands as he kissed her again with a
hungry urgency so that her heart was racing when he let

her go. There was a flush along his cheek-bones which told its own story but the flat tone of his voice chilled her.

'But it isn't just a question of what I want, is it, Abbie? It's whether or not it would be the right thing to do…in the circumstances.'

What circumstances? she wanted to cry, before it hit her like a blow what he'd meant. Nick's engagement might be over but that didn't mean he wasn't still in love with his ex-fiancée. And in his eyes it would be a betrayal of everything he felt to sleep with another woman. Maybe he could justify a few kisses but anything more was unacceptable to him.

She struggled to her feet, trying her hardest not to let him see how devastated she felt. It wasn't his fault that he didn't love her as she loved him. And it was the bitterest blow of all to be forced to admit to her feelings at this point. There would be no bells ringing for her, no shooting stars, no joy at the discovery—just the stark realisation that she loved Nick and always would. But it was an ending, not a beginning as it should have been.

'This is a fine way to get a few days off!' Sam finished bandaging her wrist then stepped back to admire his handiwork. 'There, that should do it, although I want you to have it X-rayed as soon as possible. OK?'

'Yes, all right, although I'm sure it isn't broken.' Abbie got up from the chair and looked round for her bag.

'Here you go.' Sam placed it on the end of the desk then glanced at the clock. 'Look, I'll run you over to the hospital after I've finished here. I've just got a couple more people to see and then I'm done.'

'No, I'll be fine, really. I'll get the bus or ask Jim Patterson to give me a lift when he goes to collect the kids from school. He'll be taking the school bus over there this afternoon,' she added quickly as she saw Sam open his mouth to protest.

'Well, it's up to you, but the offer's there if you want it.' He touched her lightly on the shoulder. 'At least let me run you home, Abbie. You look really shaken up.'

'I'm fine, honestly, Sam.'

She gave him a quick smile then hurried from the room, unable to cope with anything more. It was hard enough holding onto her composure as it was, and Sam's kindness threatened to be the last straw.

She made her way swiftly from the surgery via the back door, not wanting to run into any of the others on the way and be forced to explain once again what had happened. Frankly, the sooner she put the whole episode from her mind the happier she'd be!

There were quite a few cars parked in the car park and she quickly made her way between them, thinking about her own car still parked in the Delaneys' drive. She'd have to arrange for someone to collect it for her because she wouldn't be able to drive with her wrist like this. Nick had driven her to the surgery but she'd refused his offer to accompany her inside. She'd assumed that he'd left so when she suddenly spotted him parked at the end of the row it came as a shock.

'How is it?' he asked, letting down the window as she drew level with the car.

'All right. I…I need to have it X-rayed just to make sure it isn't broken,' she explained flatly, trying her hardest to keep her emotions in check.

'Jump in, then, and I'll run you over to the hospital,' he offered at once, starting the engine.

She shook her head, 'No, that isn't necessary. Sam said that he'd take me,' she added quickly as Nick frowned. It was only a small distortion of the truth because Sam *had* offered and the fact that she'd refused was by the by.

'I see.' Nick turned to stare across the car park and she heard him sigh. 'Look, Abbie, about what happened before…'

'Forget it!' She gave a discordant laugh which instantly brought his gaze back to her. Colour ran up her face and she knew that he'd seen it, but she didn't care. The only thing she was concerned about was stopping him from apologising because she couldn't bear it.

'Let's just pretend it never happened, Nick. It…it probably wasn't one of my better ideas, anyway.'

'No, it wasn't.' His face tautened as he stared at her, although she wasn't sure what she saw in his eyes. Why did he look so angry? she found herself wondering until it struck her that he probably blamed her for the way he'd almost compromised his own deep-seated sense of honour.

She turned away so that he couldn't see how much that hurt. 'Well, thanks for driving me back here. I'm sorry if I've delayed you.'

'Don't worry about it.' His tone was curt almost to the point of rudeness, and she bit her lip against the wave of pain she felt. 'Anyway I'll get off now. I want to be in London before the evening rush starts. Tell James I'll phone him tonight, will you? There might be news of Adrian by then.'

He didn't say anything more as he pulled out of the parking space. Abbie watched the car turn into the road and disappear from sight with a heavy heart. Nick was driving down to London? Why? What for? To…to see Jill and try to sort things out with her?

It was the logical explanation and made sense of how he'd reacted just now. Nick obviously deeply regretted that for a few moments he'd actually wanted another woman…

Or was she just flattering herself by thinking that? Had Nick really wanted her? Or had she been merely a substitute for the woman he loved? Had he pretended that it was

Jill in his arms, Jill's lips he was kissing with such hunger? No wonder he felt so bad about it now! But he couldn't feel nearly as bad as she did, knowing what a fool she'd been.

CHAPTER ELEVEN

'THAT was the police on the phone. It's almost a week since Adrian went missing and there's been no sign of him. They're convinced that he must have left the area by now.'

James came back into the staffroom. They'd been having an impromptu meeting to discuss the final arrangements for the computer launch, which was being held that evening, when he'd been called away. He sat down again and sighed. 'I think they're right. Someone would have seen him if he'd still been around, wouldn't they?'

'I'd have thought so,' Abbie agreed. 'Harry and Rose have been out scouring the countryside every day but they've drawn a blank. It seems likely that he's moved on, maybe gone back to London.'

'That's what I'm afraid of. I was speaking to Nick last night. He'd just got back from London himself and he was only saying how many youngsters there are living rough down there. It would be virtually impossible to track Adrian down. It's a crying shame, isn't it?' James said sadly. 'Anyway, back to tonight. Where have we got to?'

Abbie struggled to concentrate as Elizabeth carried on, but it was impossible to keep her mind on track—not that it had been easy to concentrate on anything for days now. She kept going over and over what had happened in the conservatory even though she knew how foolish it was—

She jumped as Sam nudged her, colouring when she found everyone's eyes on her. 'Sorry, I was miles away. What was that?'

'I was just wondering if you could pick up some paper plates on your way here tonight,' Elizabeth explained. 'Mrs

Lewis has decided that we can't possibly offer everyone just wine and cheese so she spent all yesterday baking. From the look of the kitchen this morning, it's going to turn into a full buffet!'

'Better make sure you buy a large pack, then,' David put in with a grin. 'Once folk know that Mrs Lewis is doing the catering we'll have queues outside the door!'

Everyone laughed but it was certainly true that Elizabeth's elderly housekeeper was a renowned cook. Abbie waited until the din died down. 'I'll fetch a couple of large packs so that should see us through. Anything else we need while I'm at it?' She glanced at her bandaged wrist and grimaced. 'It's the least I can do because I've not been much help recently.'

'Oh, I'd enjoy the rest while you can.' Sam winked at the others. 'We'll make sure that you make up for it as soon as it's better.'

'Thanks!' Abbie aimed a playful cuff at his ear as everyone laughed. 'You soon find out who your friends are, don't you? Anyway, is there anything else we need?'

Elizabeth ran through the list once more then shook her head. 'Nope, that's it. All we need now is for people to turn up and we're away.'

'Oh, I don't think there'll be much problem about folk turning up. Apart from the promise of free wine and food, everyone is keen to see how the new video link works,' James put in. 'You did arrange for someone to be at the hospital so we can demonstrate it?'

'I did, indeed,' David assured him. 'Laura's going to be there and she'll link up with us at around eight o'clock.'

'Great! Sounds as though everything is sorted, doesn't it?' Abbie glanced at her watch and quickly got to her feet. 'I'll have to go. I want to catch Sophie Jackson before she leaves. She's got her interview at the college this afternoon.'

'It's her last day for a home visit, isn't it?' Elizabeth queried, getting up as well. 'She'll be bringing William to clinic from now on?'

'Yes. I want to explain all that to her—make sure she understands how important it is and how vital it is that William has his vaccinations.' Abbie smiled ruefully. 'Annie was always a bit lax about having the children vaccinated and I don't want Sophie thinking it doesn't really matter.'

'Oh, I think Annie's had a change of heart since little Chloe was so ill,' James assured her. 'I'm sure she realises now that the vaccinations are vital.'

'You're probably right but I want to check anyway. I'll see you all tonight, then. And I won't forget the plates!'

Abbie left the surgery and walked briskly through the town to the Jacksons' house. She hadn't been able to drive since the accident or do any calls that demanded any degree of dexterity. It had been a nuisance, to say the least, but it should only be another day or so before her wrist was strong enough to let her get back to work properly.

She was looking forward to it because while she was working at least she could concentrate on something other than the thoughts which plagued both her waking and sleeping hours. It should have helped that she hadn't seen Nick but it was the reason he wasn't in town which had been so hard to accept.

Had he managed to work things out with Jill? she wondered for the hundredth time before she sighed. It wasn't any of her business if he had!

Sophie looked flustered when she opened the door. 'Come in. William's in the front room. I'm just getting him ready to take him over to Trisha's,' she explained, quickly leading the way. 'Trisha's got a free afternoon so she's going to mind him for me because Mum's had to take Chloe to the hospital for a check-up.'

'Oh, that's better than you having to cart him along on the bus, isn't it?' Abbie said, bending to look at the baby, who was lying on his changing mat and gurgling away happily. 'Hello, sweetie. How are you today?'

William grabbed her finger, hanging onto it with his chubby little fist as he smiled gummily at her, and she laughed. 'Oh, you're going to be a real heartbreaker, aren't you?'

Sophie unfolded a clean sleepsuit, groaning as she tried to slip it on him while he kicked his plump little legs about. 'He hates having his clothes on. I'm never going to get him ready at this rate.'

'Here, let me help,' Abbie offered, gently capturing the baby's flailing hands. She played pat-a-cake with him to distract his attention while Sophie slid him into the snug little outfit. She added a hand-knitted cardigan over the top with a matching hat, then popped him into a quilted sleeping bag and tucked him up in his pram.

Once again Abbie was struck by the young girl's competence but, then, Sophie had had a lot more experience with babies than the average teenager, having four younger brothers and sisters.

'Right, I won't keep you, Sophie. I just wanted to make sure that you know you can ring me any time you need to. And that William will need to be seen at baby clinic from now on to be weighed and checked over.'

'Yes, I know. Mum's said that she'll take him if I'm in college. When will he need his first injections?' she asked, hurriedly packing nappies and a change of baby clothes into a carrier bag.

'When he's about two months old. You'll be given all the details at the clinic. They really are important so do make sure that he has them, won't you?'

'Oh, I'll make certain he does,' Sophie assured her.

'Right, I'd better be on my way, then. I don't want to be late. Thanks very much for coming every day, Abbie.'

'That's quite all right, love. You just take care of yourself and that lovely baby. And good luck with your interview!'

They left the house together. Abbie watched Sophie pushing the pram down the road and felt confident that things would work out all right in the end. It wouldn't be easy for Sophie but she'd manage somehow.

Would her own life have turned out differently if she'd had the courage to do what Nick had wanted her to do all those years before? she wondered suddenly.

It was impossible to know the answer to that and futile to dwell on it. It was the present that mattered now, not the past.

'I didn't think this many would turn up!' Elizabeth looked round the crowded room and grimaced. 'I only hope we have enough wine for everyone!'

'We'll have to send out for more if not. Anyway, most people seem more interested in the food—not that I blame them. Mrs Lewis has outdone herself tonight,' Abbie replied with a laugh, looking at the laden tables.

'I'd go and grab something while you can, then,' Elizabeth advised her. 'I'll just go and see where James is.'

She headed off across the room while Abbie made her way to the end of the buffet queue, stopping several times to speak to people *en route*. She noticed Len and Mary Parker on the fringes of the crowd and made a detour to speak to them, appreciating the fact that they'd bothered to come all the way into town.

'Hello, there. How are you, Len?'

'Oh, a lot better, I'm glad to say. I don't think you've met my wife, Mary, have you?' Len said, drawing forward the pleasant-looking woman at his side. 'This is Nurse Fraser, Mary.'

'Oh, make that Abbie, please!' Abbie laughed, shaking hands with the older woman.

'I'm delighted to meet you, Abbie,' Mary Parker replied with a warm smile. 'I wanted to thank you for putting my name forward for the physiotherapy work. Dr Ross told me that it was you who suggested me for the job and I'm really grateful.'

'Oh, don't mention it. To be honest, you're doing us a favour. So many of our patients miss out on physio because of the distance involved in travelling to the hospital,' Abbie said quickly.

'It was still good of you to think of me,' Mary insisted. 'I only said as much to Mr Delaney this afternoon.'

Abbie's heart skipped a beat at the mention of Nick's name. She couldn't help herself from asking about him even though she knew it was foolish to keep torturing herself this way. 'How is Nick? He didn't overdo things in London I hope?'

Mary grimaced. 'He seemed very tired, to tell the truth. Oh, he's made excellent progress but it's early days yet and he needs to pace himself. Still, I suppose he needed to get everything sorted out for when he moves back there. There are all the modifications which need doing to his flat for starters, although fortunately there's someone there to oversee the work so he won't need to go back and forth all the time.'

'I...I see.' She wasn't sure how she managed to keep smiling. 'When is he thinking of moving back?'

'I'm not sure. Oh, but here he is so we can ask him,' Mary replied with a smile as she looked past her. 'Hello, there. We were just talking about you.'

'Something nice, I hope,' Nick replied evenly, manoeuvring his chair alongside Len and smiling around at them. His gaze rested only for a moment on Abbie, before moving on, but it was long enough. She lifted her glass to her lips and took a sip of the orange juice without tasting it. The look he'd given her had been so cool that it had hurt, yet what had she expected? He felt nothing for her except perhaps friendship rekindled from the ashes of their childhood closeness. The fact that she wanted more than that was something *she* had to deal with.

'I was just telling Abbie that you're moving back to London and she wanted to know when you were going,' Mary explained.

'By the end of the month, hopefully.' Nick turned to her and his expression was hard to read all of a sudden. 'I thought it was time I got on with my life again.'

'I...I'm pleased for you, Nick,' she said softly, struggling to keep any hint of what she was feeling out of her voice. 'I take it that you're going back to work?'

'Yes. Everything's arranged. I'd have liked to get back there sooner but there are modifications which need doing to the flat. They'll take a couple of weeks and then I'll be able to return permanently,' he explained in that same coolly polite tone.

'I see. Well, it seems that things are working out for you, aren't they?' It was an effort to smile but she forced herself not to show how devastated she felt. Nick had made no mention of Jill but that didn't mean she wasn't very much a part of his future plans. Who else would be living in the flat and supervising the alterations?

'Well, I'm really pleased for you, Mr Delaney, although I'll be sorry to lose my best patient. Not everyone works as hard as you've been doing, but, then, you've had a real incentive, haven't you?' Mary stated, oblivious to the anguish she was causing.

Nick's reasons for trying so hard to get his life back together were obvious, Abbie thought dully. He'd wanted to convince his ex-fiancée that he still had a lot to offer, and obviously it had worked. Now they had a future to

look forward to together. It just proved how great the power
of love really was.

'Oh, I'm sure you'll have many more patients to work
with,' Nick said smoothly. 'I believe there's talk of you
holding a clinic here in the surgery?'

'That's right,' Len put in proudly. 'Dr Ross has asked
Mary if she'd be willing to see any patients who need referring for physio.'

'I was thrilled to be asked,' Mary added. 'I've told Dr
Ross that I'm happy to do home visits as well for those
who can't get into town.'

'Then you're going to need a little car to get about,' Len
stated firmly. 'I'm not having you waiting around for the
bus, not after seeing that young fellow who's been hanging
about all the time. Looked a bit strange to me, he did.'

'Oh, I don't expect there's any harm in him, Len. Don't
fuss so. I've dealt with far worse than him when I was
working at the hospital!' Mary assured him with a laugh.

'Well, I'm glad that things are working out so well for
you here,' Nick said sincerely. 'Yewdale is a nice place to
live, isn't it, Abbie?'

She'd thought so once but suddenly she knew that, living
and working here, it wasn't going to be the same once Nick
had gone. Her heart was breaking but somehow she managed to smile. 'It is. I...I'm sure you'll be happy here,
Mary.'

There must have been something in her voice because
she saw Nick frown, but suddenly she knew that she
couldn't take any more. It was a relief when their attention
was diverted by a sudden commotion in the hallway. She
looked round and was surprised to see Sophie Jackson, sur-
rounded by a small group of people. Frank and Jeannie
Shepherd were there, looking extremely worried, as well as
Barry Jackson, who looked very grim. Young Billy Murray
was also there and he looked really upset.

She quickly excused herself and hurried out to see what was wrong. 'What's the matter?' she asked just as David and Sam appeared to see what was going on.

'Is Trisha here?' Sophie demanded before anyone else could speak.

'Trisha? No, I haven't seen her.' She glanced at the other two, who shook their heads. 'She hasn't been here tonight. Why are you looking for her? What's happened?'

'I…I went to Trisha's to collect William when I got back from town. I missed the bus, you see, and had to wait over an hour for the next one so I was really late. When I got to her house there was nobody in so I thought she must have got fed up waiting and taken William home, but my mum hasn't seen her. Nobody seems to know where she is or what's happened to my baby!' Sophie wailed, her voice rising hysterically.

Abbie took hold of her arm and quickly led her into one of the consulting rooms and sat her down on a chair, before turning to Jeannie Shepherd. 'And you haven't any idea where Trisha has gone?'

'No. I was at work this afternoon, you see. Oh, I knew she'd arranged to look after the baby so when she wasn't in when I got home I just thought she must have gone over to Sophie's with him. Frank's been at his dad's all day and only got back a short time ago. We were just getting ourselves ready to come here when Sophie arrived.' Jeannie's voice broke. 'I…I don't know what's happened to our Trisha!'

'I'll ring Mike to see if he's seen her,' David said immediately, picking up the phone. Everyone waited in silence while he spoke quietly to his son. Abbie suddenly realised that Nick had joined them but she avoided looking in his direction, focusing solely on what was happening.

David's face was set when he put the phone down. 'Mike hasn't seen her. They were supposed to be working together on some assignment for college but she didn't show up. He was just on his way over to your house, Jeannie, to see what had happened to her when I phoned. He said he'll ring round their friends and check if anyone has seen her and get back to me.'

'It isn't like her!' Frank exclaimed suddenly. 'Our Trisha has a sight more sense than to go off like this, especially with a baby. Something's up, I know it. I'm going to see if I can find her.'

'I'll come with you,' Billy said at once, hurrying after the older man.

'So will I,' Sam stated, going over to join them. 'I'll take my mobile so as soon as you hear anything phone me. OK?'

The three of them set off together. Sam must have stopped to have a word with James on the way out because he came in to speak to them.

Nick was talking quietly to Sophie, holding her hand as she sat sobbing in the chair. His very posture exuded reassurance and Abbie was suddenly glad that he was there. Nick was someone people would turn to in a time of crisis, someone they would listen to and draw comfort from. It made her feel proud even though there was no reason for her to feel that way.

'What do you think has happened?' James asked once they'd moved out of earshot. 'Trisha doesn't strike me as the sort of girl to cause such an upset.'

'She isn't,' Abbie replied emphatically. 'Trisha's very level-headed and responsible. She wouldn't dream of upsetting everyone like this.'

'Then we have to assume that something has happened to her,' David stated bluntly, voicing all their fears. 'The thing that springs to mind is some sort of problem brought on by her diabetes. Let's see if Jeannie remembers her taking her insulin for starters.'

Jeannie was adamant that her daughter had given herself an injection that morning. 'I always check just to be sure. It drives her mad, me asking all the time if she's remembered, but I still do it.' She put a hand to her mouth to hold back a sob. 'She'll need another one soon. She has one at eight in the morning and another at eight in the evening. What's going to happen if she misses it? She'd be ill, wouldn't she, maybe go into a…a coma? You have to find her!'

'We will, Jeannie. We'll find her. But maybe Trisha has taken her insulin with her. Did you check?' Abbie asked, trying to keep her calm.

'I never thought to look. I should have done but I was that scared, you see…' Jeannie trailed off.

Abbie squeezed her hand. 'It's understandable.'

'I'll give Sam a ring and ask him to get Frank to check if Trisha has her insulin kit with her,' James said quietly. 'Then I think we'd better give the police a call. I don't think we can afford to waste any time on this.'

Nobody said anything but Abbie knew that the same thought must be going through all their minds. If Trisha didn't have the necessary injection of insulin with her then she could fall ill. She might not recognise the warning signs and realise that any dizziness and confusion was the onset of hypoglycaemia.

Had she explained to Trisha how important it was that she carried something sugary with her at all times to ward off such an attack? She thought she had but she couldn't be certain that the girl would have remembered.

Jeannie started crying as James picked up the phone to make the calls. Abbie put her arm around her. 'Try not to worry, Jeannie. Trisha will be fine. And so will William,' she added as Sophie began sobbing again. 'Trisha won't let anything happen to him, love. You know that.'

Her eyes met Nick's over the top of the girl's head and

she saw her own fears reflected in them. Under normal circumstances Trisha would take great care of the baby, but if she'd been taken ill then she might not be in a position to do so.

There didn't seem much anyone could do until the police arrived. Abbie went to the staffroom and put the kettle on to make everyone a cup of tea. She stared out of the window while she waited for it to come to the boil. It was pitch black outside, the wind carrying flurries of rain down from the mountains.

At this time of the year it got very cold at night and anyone caught out in the open ran the risk of exposure. Trisha was seriously at risk if she were lying unconscious somewhere and she didn't dare think what might happen to baby William.

'They'll be all right, Abbie. We'll find them.'

Nick brought the chair to a stop beside her and reached for her hand. He gave her cold fingers a gentle squeeze. Abbie stared out the window as tears burned her eyes. She ached for the comfort of his strong arms around her at that moment, longed to have him hold her close and tell her that things would turn out all right, but it was too much to ask. She didn't have the right to expect anything more than this token of friendship from him.

'I hope so, Nick.' She drew her hand from his and he didn't try to stop her as she moved away. When he turned and left the room she felt tears run down her face. She'd never felt more alone than she did at that moment.

'We'll make our base here. Someone needs to man the phones so that we can keep a check on which areas have been covered.'

Mark Winters, the leader of the local mountain rescue team, looked round the group assembled in the surgery. The police had enlisted his help in the search for Trisha and the baby and it was some comfort to have him take charge.

'I'll do that,' Abbie offered immediately. She shot a glance at her bandaged arm and grimaced. 'I'd like to go out and look for her but I'd be more hindrance than help.'

'I'll stay as well,' Nick put in. 'There's little I can do apart from drive around in the car. If Trisha's been taken ill close to the road someone would have found her by now.'

'Fine. You'll need to liaise with Ian Farnsworth's wife over at the Outward Bound centre. His team's covering the area round Yewdale Water,' Mark explained, quickly showing him the area on the map. 'It seems unlikely that the girl would have got very far with a baby in tow but, as you said, Nick, someone should have spotted her if she'd been by a main road. We can't afford to overlook the possibility that she may have become confused and wandered further afield.'

'Sam's group is scouring the town,' James put in. 'They've got together with some of the other men and are checking any outbuildings, sheds, that sort of thing.'

'And Mike and Danny have gone over to the church with the police to check that area,' David added. 'The last sighting of Trisha had her heading that way. Marion Rimmer saw her pushing the baby along when she went to the cemetery to put flowers on her husband's grave.'

'It's the only lead we have so far.' Elizabeth sighed. 'I never thought I'd say this but thank heavens that Marion is so nosy!'

They all laughed but it was only a momentary relief—everyone was becoming increasingly concerned as time passed. Abbie looked around after the search party left. The celebrations had broken up as soon as people had heard about Trisha's disappearance and the remains of the buffet was still on the table. Most of the town was anxious to help

in any way they could and there were groups out everywhere, looking for the girl.

'You feel so damned useless sitting here when you want
to be out there, helping,' Nick stated as he swung the chair
round to look out of the window.

'You do. Is it still raining?' she asked, trying to keep her
tone even. Now that everyone had left she was very much
aware that they were on their own. It was going to be a
strain, getting through the hours, but she had to put aside
her own feelings and get on with it.

'Harder than ever. Damn!' he swore impatiently as he
turned the chair back round. 'I should have gone along
anyway. I could have checked some of the side streets or
driven over to Newthwaite or something.'

'They need someone here to co-ordinate things, Nick.
You know that. It's better that you stayed.'

'Rather than got in the way, you mean?' He laughed
harshly. 'Always blunt and to the point, eh, Abbie? Still,
it's better I accept my limitations and get on with life, rather
than wishing for the impossible.'

She wasn't sure what he meant or why he sounded so
angry. It was on the tip of her tongue to ask but she stopped
herself. She began to collect up the paper plates and put
them in a refuse sack. The phone rang and Nick answered
it, shrugging as he hung up.

'Just Barbara Farnsworth to say that the area around the
Outward Bound centre is clear. Ian has taken his group
along the east shore of the lake now and she'll report back
later.'

It was a long night and the tension increased as each
report came in and there was still no sign of Trisha. Abbie
and Nick drank endless cups of coffee as they waited for
news. Neither of them seemed inclined to talk much, probably because they weren't sure what to say to one another.

What had happened in the conservatory had been a turning point for both of them probably.

Had it helped Nick crystallise his feelings for Jill as it had helped her realise how she felt about him? Abbie wondered sadly. Maybe.

James and Elizabeth were first to arrive back at around midnight, looking worn out. However, they insisted that she go home and try to get some sleep as they'd cover the phones. Abbie didn't want to leave but when Nick added his voice to the argument she gave in. Maybe he, too, had been aware that the tension hadn't stemmed solely from the situation they were dealing with.

Rain was sweeping across the town and the temperature seemed to have dropped by several degrees as she made her way home. She passed several groups of searchers on the way but they had nothing to report. She turned wearily into her road, wondering where Trisha was. Yewdale wasn't a very big place and it seemed inconceivable that anyone could disappear like that. But, then, look how Adrian had gone missing…

The thought was like a starburst. It seemed to set off flashes in her mind. Adrian peering through the Shepherds' kitchen window that day; Trisha's belief that he was following her; those photographs taped to his dressing-table mirror; what Len Parker had said about seeing a vagrant in the area.

She ran up the path and let herself into the house. Her hands were shaking so hard that it took her three attempts to dial Directory Enquiries and interminable seconds before they supplied the Parkers' phone number. Len answered after half a dozen rings, sounding as though she'd dragged him out of bed.

'It's Abbie Fraser, Len. Look, I haven't time to explain but where did you see that man hanging around? It's really important.'

'Well, I've seen him a few times now but mainly around that old house a couple of miles from here. I did wonder if he was sleeping rough there as I've seen smoke coming from the place.'

'Do you mean the old Harper property?' Abbie demanded eagerly.

'Yes, that's it. I mentioned it to Mr Walsh and I'm sure that's what he called the place. Do you know it, then?'

'I do. Thanks, Len. Look, can I ask you a favour? Will you ring the surgery and tell them that I think I know where Trisha might be? Tell them that I think she's with Adrian at the old Harper property and that I'm going straight over there? Have you got that?'

'Yes, of course. But don't you think you should wait for someone to go with you? I didn't like the look of that young fellow at all,' Len said, sounding worried.

'If it's Adrian then he knows me. It'll be all right,' she assured him with more confidence than she actually felt. But every extra minute's delay simply increased the risk to Trisha and the baby.

She hung up and went in search of her car keys then let herself out of the house. Her wrist protested as she pulled away from the kerb but she ignored it as she drove quickly out of town. It took her a good fifteen minutes to reach the overgrown track leading to the derelict farmhouse, and even then she almost overshot the turning.

She slowed down to a crawl as she eased the car over the ruts. Trees overhung the track on both sides, scraping against the car roof as she made her way slowly to the farmhouse. It was pitch black this far from the road and her headlights bounced back off the dense undergrowth so that it was difficult to see where she was going. It was a relief when the house came into sight at last and she was able to stop.

She took a good look around, wondering if she was mad

to think anyone was living there. The place had been abandoned for years and large sections of the roof had caved in, leaving it open to the elements. It seemed unlikely that Adrian could have spent the past week there but she had to check.

She got out of the car, leaving the headlights on so that she could see where she was going. There was no sound apart from the rustle of the bushes as the wind whipped through them. She'd just decided that Len had been mistaken when she suddenly caught the scent of woodsmoke. She crept to the door, holding her breath as she peered inside…

Trisha was sitting huddled up in a corner of what had been the living-room before the house had been abandoned. She was holding the baby in her arms and crying softly as she rocked him. She looked up as she heard Abbie's footsteps and her face broke into a smile of relief which changed almost immediately to an expression of horror.

'No, don't…don't!'

Abbie swung round and her heart seemed to stop as she saw the figure behind her. It was a second before she realised that it was Adrian because he was so unkempt. He took a slow step towards her and her eyes dropped from his face to the knife he was holding. Suddenly she knew that it had been the biggest mistake of her life, coming here on her own!

CHAPTER TWELVE

'THEY sent you, didn't they? They sent you to take her away from me!'

There was a sing-song quality to Adrian's voice which chilled her. Abbie's hands clenched as she tried to work out what to do but it was impossible to deal rationally with a situation like this. She just had to trust her instincts and pray that they wouldn't let her down.

'Nobody sent me, Adrian. I came because I wanted to make sure that Trisha and the baby were all right. I'm a nurse and it's my job to take care of people.'

'She doesn't need you taking care of her! I'm going to do that. I'm going to take her and the baby some place *they* can't find us!'

He took a threatening step towards her. Abbie backed away, careful not to take her eyes off him. Trisha was sobbing in the background and the baby was starting to grizzle as he sensed her fear. Adrian shot a glance at them and frowned.

'Why are you crying? You know we want to be together. Nobody can stop us now, you'll see.'

'I don't know what he means!' Trisha wailed. 'He's crazy!'

'Try to stay calm, Trisha,' Abbie said quickly, trying to suppress her own fear because she knew how important it was that they did nothing to exacerbate the situation.

How long would it be before anyone else got here? she wondered sickly. Len would have phoned the surgery straight away but it could take time to contact the police and get them over here. In the meantime, she had to concentrate on keeping everything calm, and if Trisha became hysterical that would be impossible.

'Is it all right if I sit down?' she asked Adrian, her tone as unthreatening as she could make it. 'Trisha must be tired, holding the baby all the time, so maybe I can hold him while she has a rest?'

He seemed to weigh up the dangers of what she'd suggested before he nodded, although his eyes never left her as she sat down beside the terrified teenager.

'Shall I take William now, love?' she asked softly. Under cover of handing the baby over, she gave Trisha's hand a reassuring squeeze, wishing someone could do the same for her. Unbidden, her mind went back to those moments in the surgery when Nick had held her hand, and she ached for him then with an intensity which was painful before she made herself put it from her mind. Nick couldn't help her at the moment. It was up to her to do all she could to keep them safe.

'How are you feeling, Trisha?' she asked softly, keeping a wary eye on Adrian, who was pacing the floor and muttering to himself now.

'I'm OK, I think. I felt odd before, sort of dizzy and woolly-headed, but I had a can of Coke with me so I drank that and it helped. I...I'm just so scared, Abbie. What does he want with me?'

'It'll be all right, love. Just try to stay calm...'

'What are you whispering about? You think I don't know what you're trying to do?' Adrian took a threatening step towards her. Abbie forced herself to stay quite still and not show how scared she was. He looked so wild and unkempt that his appearance was warning enough of how far his state of mind had deteriorated. One wrong look or word and it could have disastrous consequences for all of them.

He glared at her for a moment longer then spun round and started pacing again. Abbie let out her pent-up breath but she was shaking as she settled the fussy baby more comfortably in her arms. She cast a glance at her watch, working out how long it had taken her to get there and how long it would be before help arrived. Let someone come soon! she prayed. She wasn't sure how long she could stall Adrian if he decided it was time to leave.

The thought had barely crossed her mind when she heard a noise outside, although she hadn't heard a vehicle driving up. Adrian swung round like an animal at bay, the knife gripped in his hand as he stared towards the door. Abbie bit her lip to contain her gasp of shock as Nick suddenly appeared. How he'd got over the rutted ground in the wheelchair she had no idea, but suddenly he was there and she almost cried out in relief at seeing him.

'Hello, Adrian. My name is Nick. Do you mind if I come in?' His tone was gentle and betrayed no hint of fear even though he must have seen the knife in the boy's hand. It obviously threw Adrian because he stepped back as Nick carefully propelled the wheelchair into the room.

He shot a look over to the corner where Abbie and Trisha were huddled and his eyes met hers for the briefest of moments before he looked away, but what she'd seen in them made her head spin.

Was she going crazy? Or had Nick just looked at her as though she were the most precious thing in the whole world?

What happened next was forever a blur in her mind. She was conscious of Nick's quiet voice speaking to the boy for what seemed like ages. When Adrian handed over the knife to him she wept with relief, but it was relief for all of them. Adrian needed help and, scary though it had been, he couldn't be held responsible for what had happened.

Suddenly the house seemed to be full of police. David and James were there as well, David bending to put a comforting arm round a sobbing Trisha while James took the baby from her. Sam was there, too, helping her to her feet and hugging her hard.

'Are you OK, Abbie?'

'I think so…' She managed a smile. 'Remind me not to go doing anything like this again, will you?'

'What's that saying about fools rushing in?' he teased, but she could see the strain on his face.

'I might have known you'd come up with that…' she began, then tailed off as Nick suddenly appeared at her side. She wasn't even aware of Sam letting her go and moving away as she stared at him.

'Don't ever do anything like this to me again!' His voice grated with such emotion that it brought her heart to a stop.

She took a deep breath and then another for good measure, but neither helped. Nick was looking at her with his heart in his eyes and she couldn't seem to take it in. He loved her? He couldn't do! It was Jill he loved, Jill he wanted to spend his life with! So why was he looking at *her* like that? a small voice jeered.

'Let's get out of here.' His tone was still curt as he spun the chair round, but Abbie found herself obeying without question. David said something to her and she responded, but she had no idea what she'd said as she followed Nick from the house. There was a line of cars drawn up in the lane and Nick's was at the very front, right behind hers. He swore softly as he realised that they were blocked in by the other vehicles.

'Here.' Sam had followed them outside and he tossed Abbie the keys to his car, which was at the very back of the line. 'Take my car. I'd say your need is greater than mine at this moment!'

She blushed as she saw the knowing grin on his face but she didn't refuse the offer. Nick didn't say a word as they made their way to the car nor did he speak after they'd finally got him in and loaded his chair into the boot. She shot a look at him as she started the engine, feeling the quiver that ran through her as he suddenly turned.

'I told myself that I was going to do what was right, Abbie. But, so help me, I need you—no matter if it's selfish or not!'

'Nick, I—'

She got no further as he leaned across the seat and kissed her with a hunger and passion that robbed her of the ability to think of anything but how much she loved him. He drew back and there was a shimmer of tears in his eyes he didn't try to hide.

'I love you, Abbie. I let you go once because I thought it was best for you but I can't let you go again.'

'Oh, Nick, I love you, too!' She put her arms around his neck and clung to him, murmuring as he showered kisses over her eyelids and temples then let his lips drift down to find hers again. The kiss promised to go on for some time until a tap on the window brought them apart.

Abbie blushed as the police officer blandly asked if she'd mind moving the car as nobody else could move until she did.

Nick chuckled wickedly as she clashed the gears then hurriedly backed up the lane. 'Hmm, in trouble with the law now, Nurse Fraser? Seems like you're having yourself quite a night.'

She shot him a grin as she turned onto the road and headed back towards Yewdale. 'And it isn't over yet...I hope!'

He lifted her hand from the steering-wheel and kissed her fingers one by one, laughing softly when she gasped. 'We'll have to see what we can arrange, won't we?'

Moonlight poured through the window, casting delicate shadows over the room. By unspoken consent they hadn't turned on any lights, and the silvery wash of colour added a touch of magic to the scene. Odd that after that first urgency there seemed to be no reason to rush. They had all the time in the world to make this night special.

'Come here.' Nick's voice was soft, in keeping with the dream-like quality of the moment. Abbie went and knelt in front of him, closing her eyes as he sculpted her face with kisses. His lips were cool against her skin, gentle and tender too, yet she sensed the hunger which was held in check for the moment. A shiver ran through her as she wondered how it would feel when it was finally unleashed. But for now there was no reason to rush, no need to hurry.

His hand slid along her jaw, caressing, stroking, moving on to glide down her neck, and she gave a tiny murmur of pleasure and felt him smile against her mouth. When his fingers moved to the buttons on her lemon silk blouse she held her breath, her pulse racing as he worked them free then followed the route his fingers had travelled with his lips.

His mouth came to rest on the shadowy hollow between her breasts and she murmured again as she felt his warm breath on her skin. Reaching round behind her, she unclipped her bra and let the straps slide down her arms, hearing the groan he gave as her full breasts were suddenly bared to his gaze.

'You're beautiful, Abbie…so very beautiful.' His voice shook with emotion but his hands were steady as he cupped her breasts to lavish each rigid nipple with the attention it craved.

Abbie let her head drop back and closed her eyes as the sensations swept through her like wine. It was quiet in the room with just the whispery sound of her breathing and the rougher sound of his to fill the silence, and they were a stimulant in themselves. How she ached for the feel of his mouth on her, yearned for an even greater closeness…

He made a small murmur of protest as she moved then

stilled as her hands went to the front of his shirt. His eyes were dark and glittering as they watched her while she unfastened the tiny buttons, one by one, slowly...

'You know, you could drive me crazy, doing that,' he grated, making no attempt to stop her.

'Could I?' She slid her hand through the gap in the cotton, letting her fingers move lightly over the smooth, hard flesh and tangle in the crisp dark hair, and heard the smothered groan he gave.

There was a heady ring to her soft laughter when he pushed her hands away and undid the last few buttons himself then slipped the shirt off his shoulders, but it changed in an instant to a moan of desire as he caught her around the waist and drew her to him so that her breasts were pressed against the hard, warm muscles in his chest.

Abbie drew in a shaky lungful of air as the room seemed to spin in a dizzying spiral. 'That's not fair,' she whispered, her voice betraying all the rawness of emotion she felt. 'Now you're driving me crazy.'

'We're driving each other crazy, my darling.' His mouth was hungry as he kissed her with a thoroughness that made it hard for her to think straight. He tilted her face so that he could look deep into her eyes and she saw the shadow which haunted the depths of his. 'I want to make love to you, Abbie, so much that it hurts, but I'm not sure if I can. W-will you help me?'

Her voice broke as she realised how much it must have cost him to ask, but it just made her love him even more. 'You know I will, Nick. Just as you must know that even if it doesn't work this time it won't change how I feel about you. I love you, and we have all the time in the world to make this come right.'

He kissed her again with a delicacy that didn't disguise his hunger and relief. She kissed him back, letting him know from her response how much she loved him and how willing she was to help. His eyes followed her as she stood up and slowly took off the rest of her clothes then helped him remove the rest of his.

The old settee was big enough to hold them both as they lay side by side, Nick's arms cradling her against him, his body pressed all down the length of hers so that she could feel the hardness of his muscles against her softness. That was sensuous enough without the way his hands stroked her skin, bringing to life all the tiny pulse points. She was trembling with desire when he drew her above him and smiled at her with eyes dark with love and desire.

'I think this is going to work after all,' he muttered just a moment before their bodies made the final adjustment and proved him right. And then there was no need for any more words or doubts as they were both swept away by the magic of their love.

'Six out of ten for the technical merit but twenty out of ten for sheer pleasure!'

Nick grinned as he drew her closer, looking so overwhelmingly male and smug that Abbie laughed.

'And I bet I know who's responsible for which!' she teased. 'I'm the technical merit and you're...'

'Pleasure!' He kissed her hard and extremely thoroughly, not at all abashed by the claim. Abbie knew that it was true because Nick had been the one to guide her so that their love-making had been more wonderful than she could have dared hope. He'd been so tender and patient as he'd taught her what to do so that any shyness she'd felt had soon disappeared.

'It was wonderful, Nick,' she said softly. 'I never expected anything could feel like that.'

'So you weren't disappointed?' There was a sudden uncertainty in his voice and she hurried to reassure him.

'No! I...I never felt like that before, if you want the truth.'

'Not even with your husband?' He shrugged, trying to make light of the question, although she knew deep down that it was important to him to hear the answer. 'You don't have to answer that, Abbie. I don't mean to pry.'

'You aren't prying. And the answer is just the same. I never felt like that with Paul, never wanted him as I want you. I never really loved him, you see, Nick, and that's what makes all the difference in the world.'

'God, what fools we've been, wasting all these years!' He sighed, pressing his face into her hair. 'If there's anything I regret then it's that, Abbie.'

'Don't, Nick. Don't spoil what we have now by looking back. You can't change the past and there are some things I don't think either of us would want to change,' she added softly.

'You mean your daughter, Megan, don't you?' He understood at once what she'd meant and her heart swelled with love for him.

'Yes, I don't regret having Megan. How could I? She was the one good thing that came out of my marriage, and in the few months I had her she gave me so much joy,' she admitted quietly.

'I wish I'd seen her, Abbie. I wish I'd been there and held her just once because she was such an important part of your life.' There was a catch in his voice and she kissed him quickly, touched by what he'd said—by his unstinting generosity. That Megan had been another man's child made no difference to Nick because he still shared her grief for the child's loss. It was what made him what he was, what made her love him so much.

'I wish you'd seen her, too, Nick. You'd have loved her, I'm sure. But maybe one day we can have a child of our own, not to replace Megan but to love for its own sake,' she suggested tentatively, not sure how he'd react to the idea.

'I hope so, darling! I can't think of anything I'd like more than to know you were carrying our child,' he said fiercely.

'But you told me that you didn't care that Jill didn't want a family,' she couldn't help but say in surprise.

'And it was true. Children simply weren't part of the equation where Jill and I were concerned.' He sighed as he smoothed a tumbled lock of hair back from her cheek.

'I don't know how to explain it but my relationship with Jill was as much for convenience as anything else. She's a beautiful, intelligent woman and we got on well. It seemed the right thing to do for us to get married but it wasn't the love affair of the century by any means. And I know that Jill felt exactly the same way.'

'But you were so upset by the ending of your engagement,' she said. 'When I first saw you, you'd virtually given up, Nick.'

'I know. I don't deny it either.' He kissed away the frown lines from between her brows. 'To be honest, there didn't seem to be much left to look forward to. I'd been through so much, both mentally and physically, as a result of the accident but I don't think it was just that.

'It was also realising that I didn't give a damn if Jill married me or not which brought it home to me how little I had in my life apart from my work. And then along you came with your sharp little tongue, poking and prodding as only you can do! It certainly woke me up but it brought all sorts of problems into focus as well.'

'Problems? What do you mean? But don't think I've forgotten that dig about my "sharp little tongue", Delaney!' she threatened, glaring at him with mock severity which disappeared in a trice as he ran a lazy fingertip across the downward curve of her lips.

'Oh, I'm sure you haven't. I'm hoping you'll pay me back in a suitable manner, Nurse Fraser.' His leering smile made her laugh as he hammed things up but she wasn't blind to the desire she could see shimmering in the depths of his eyes. It was an effort to concentrate as he continued, in fact.

'Problems like realising that I was still in love with you for a start. Then the huge and seemingly unsurmountable problem of being confined to a wheelchair.' He looked away but the roughness of his voice told her how much that had plagued him.

'I promised myself that I wouldn't burden you with how I felt because I was terrified of playing on your sympathy in any way. I knew you weren't exactly immune to me after that afternoon in the pool but I couldn't be sure it wasn't just a reaction to what we'd felt for one another all those years ago.'

'But couldn't you tell I was falling in love with you all over again, Nick?' she protested.

'I didn't want to let myself believe that. What could I offer you, Abbie? You deserved more than a man who might never be able to be a proper husband to you, a man who might not be able to give you the children you wanted either. I'd be taking everything from you and giving nothing back in return. It wasn't right.'

'You don't think that now, though, Nick?' she asked shakily, her heart turning over at the thought. Her voice must have given away her fear because he drew her even closer.

'No! Maybe it's selfish in a way but I can't let you go. I can't live without you, darling. I tried to be strong, which is why I went back to London to get my life back in order. But every day I was away from you was a nightmare!' He tilted her face up.

'That day when you hurt your wrist I wanted so much

to take what you were offering me but I couldn't allow myself to do that. It didn't seem right to ruin your life. I also wasn't sure if you really understood what you were doing or if it was just generosity that prompted your offer to sleep with me.'

'I don't know how I had the nerve,' she admitted, blushing furiously as he laughed. 'All right, so you can laugh at me, but I don't usually go round propositioning men. That was the first time and not very successful either. But when you turned me down I thought it was because of Jill—that you couldn't bear to make love to another woman because you were still in love with her.'

'Nothing could have been further from the truth. Now, that's enough explanations for the moment,' he growled.

'Why? What have you got planned?' she asked innocently, then gasped as he rolled her over so that her back was pressed against the soft cushions. The kiss was long enough to make her forget everything else. He drew back and suddenly said, 'By the way, how about Adam?'

Her reply was completely honest. 'Adam who?' she asked bemusedly, and heard him laugh before his mouth found hers and the magic began all over again.

'Trisha is fine. They're releasing her from hospital later today... Well, well, and if it isn't our heroine of the hour!' David grinned as he glanced pointedly at the clock. 'Better late than never, I suppose.'

Abbie blushed furiously as everyone laughed. It was almost midday and she had no excuse for being so late into work...or at least none that she intended to share with everyone! However, it was soon obvious that the others had put two and two together and had arrived at the correct answer.

'I hope Nick's none the worse for his night's adventures,' Sam said blandly. He gave her a grin. 'I mean, the way he drove last night must have taken a few years off his life. It was a good job the police were too interested in getting to the old Harper house to write out any speeding tickets, otherwise he'd have a handful!'

'Nick's fine,' she replied with suitable decorum, not rising to the bait. 'I've just dropped him off at home and I've brought your car back as well. So, what have I missed?'

'Not much,' Elizabeth replied with a smile. 'As you probably heard, Trisha's none the worse for her escapade and William's fine. I've been round there this morning to see him and there's nothing to worry about.'

'Good. And Adrian?' Abbie asked.

'He's been re-admitted to hospital. Harry and Rose are there with him. He's quite ill but his doctors are hopeful they can get him sorted out. It's all a bit muddled but somehow he'd got it into his head that Trisha was his girlfriend and people were keeping them apart. He seemed to think that the baby was his as well, which is all rather sad,' James explained.

'Let's hope he gets the help he needs,' Abbie said quietly, her heart going out to the boy. 'How did he manage to persuade Trisha to go with him? Do you know?'

'Evidently, Sophie had forgotten to leave a bottle for the baby when she took him round to Trisha's. She gave Trisha her key so that she could go to her house and get one out of the fridge. The Jacksons' house is close to the church, as you know, so that must have been when Marion Rimmer saw her.

'Anyway, Trisha left William outside in his pram and when she came out of the house Adrian was there. He started wheeling the pram away and she ran after him. He had the knife and she was terrified he'd hurt William so she went with him,' Elizabeth explained soberly.

'It's amazing that nobody saw them,' Abbie said.

'Don't forget that Adrian grew up here and he knows all

the paths. He dumped the pram, which was found this morning, and took a back route through the fields to the old Harper house, which he'd been using.' David shrugged. 'I suppose luck was on his side because there were few people about.'

'Well, thank heavens things turned out all right in the end,' Abbie said sincerely. 'I just hope nothing like that ever happens again.'

'Oh, I think we all agree on that. Right, now the excitement is over with, we'd better get some work done,' David decided. 'I'm off to do some calls. See you all later.'

Everyone disappeared, apart from Elizabeth. 'So, is everything all right, then, with you and Nick?'

'Fine. We...we seem to have things sorted out,' Abbie replied with a smile that said everything.

Elizabeth hugged her. 'I'm so glad, Abbie! I wish you both all the luck in the world. I had a feeling that there was something going on, and when Nick took off like a bat out of hell after Len Parker phoned last night I was certain!'

'I love him so much, Liz,' she admitted softly.

'Then I don't think there's going to be a problem, do you?' She chuckled suddenly. 'Me, David, Sam and now you. Think it's a record?'

Abbie laughed. 'Maybe we should start advertising. Come to Yewdale and find romance!'

'It's a good idea. Anyway, take the rest of the day off. You deserve it, Abbie, after what you went through last night. I'm sure you can find something to do with a few spare hours, can't you?'

'Oh, I can!' She grinned as she headed for the door. 'And I know just the person I want to spend them with, too!'

EPILOGUE

'YOU look absolutely gorgeous, Liz!'

Abbie sighed as she looked at her friend, who was a vision in white satin and lace. It was the day of the wedding at last and she'd just finished helping Elizabeth get ready.

'Are you sure I look OK? It isn't too over the top…?' Elizabeth turned to look in the mirror, a frown puckering her brow as she studied her reflection.

Abbie laughed as she went over to straighten a curled-up edge of the bride's shoulder-length veil. 'You look marvellous. James is going to be one very proud and happy man when he sees you.'

'I can hardly believe it's going to happen at last!' Elizabeth laughed softly, her eyes sparkling with happiness as she met Abbie's gaze in the glass. 'And it will be your turn soon, don't forget.'

'How could I?' Abbie took a deep breath but it was impossible to contain the happiness she felt so she didn't even try. She and Nick were to be married after Christmas and it made this day even more poignant as she looked forward to the time when she'd become his wife. They'd decided to get married right here in Yewdale even though they'd be moving back to London because of Nick's work.

Abbie knew that she'd miss everyone but it was just too important, being with Nick. They'd been apart too long as it was. Come January she'd be leaving her post, and a new district nurse had been found to take over from her.

She looked round as the door suddenly opened and the two young bridesmaids came rushing in. Emily and little

Chloe Jackson looked adorable in their long blue dresses with coronets of tiny white flowers pinned to their hair.

'The car's here!' Emily announced, hardly able to contain her excitement.

'Then it's time we were on our way,' Abbie declared, laughing as the two girls went rushing out of the room again as fast as they'd arrived. 'Will they last the day at this rate, I wonder?'

Elizabeth smiled. 'Oh, I think Emily's becoming rather an old hand at this. First she was bridesmaid for her father and Laura, now me, then there's you and Nick...'

'And Sam and Holly in a couple of years' time!' Abbie finished for her, grinning.

'Uh-huh. Just think, we'll be old married women by then, won't we?' Elizabeth teased.

'Speak for yourself! OK, the married will be true but old—never!' she retorted. 'But, seriously, Liz, I want to wish you all the happiness in the world. Now, I'd better go and see what those two little horrors are up to.'

She left the room, exchanging a few words with Elizabeth's father on the way downstairs. He'd arrived home from Australia, looking fit and well despite his heart attack, and was obviously looking forward to his daughter's wedding day.

Jim Patterson opened the car door and ushered her and the two small bridesmaids into the back of the gleaming limousine. Abbie stared out of the window as they drove the short distance to the church, thinking that even the weather had been kind to them. Gloriously bright sunshine lit the mountains and dappled the town, taking the chill out of the December day.

There was a small gasp of delight from the crowd as she and the children got out of the car. Abbie smiled as she walked up the path to the church door, spotting familiar faces all along the route. Isaac Shepherd, looking unaccustomedly smart in his demob suit, was standing with Frank and Jeannie and their children. Trisha waved to her and Abbie waved back, then spotted Sophie Jackson with Billy Murray and their families. Billy's mother was holding baby William and Abbie smiled her delight at how things had worked out so happily in the end.

The shock of nearly losing the grandson they hadn't seen had had a galvanising effect on Billy's parents and they'd finally accepted the situation. She was glad for all of them because families were so important.

People were still hurrying into the church, although a few hung back to watch the bride arrive. Abbie spoke to Harvey and Helen Walsh then Tom and Mavis Roughley. It seemed that most of the town had turned out and she knew that Elizabeth would be thrilled to see so many old friends in the crowd.

A little ripple of applause broke out when Elizabeth arrived at last to walk up the path on her proud father's arm. The organist struck up the opening chords of the wedding march and then they all moved inside the church.

Abbie could see James standing at the altar with David, who was his best man, at his side. Sam was there, too, sitting next to Holly, and beside her was Laura. They looked round and Sam winked as he caught her eye.

She smiled back then let her gaze move on and felt her heart surge as her eyes finally met those of the one person she wanted to see most of all. Nick was sitting at the end of a row and he turned to watch her as she came down the aisle. His gaze never left her face and she felt her heart swell as she saw the expression in his eyes, all the love he made no attempt to hide.

Her hand brushed his shoulder as she passed him—just the lightest of touches which nobody but them noticed. It was a promise and a token of their commitment. One day soon they, too, would make their vows here in this church. One day they would be joined as man and wife at last.

As a brilliant ray of sunshine suddenly poured through the window behind the altar and fell on them, Abbie knew that she'd found everything she'd ever wanted right here in this town, and that at some point in the future she'd come back here. It wasn't really the end of the story.

MILLS & BOON®
MEDICAL ROMANCE™

HER PASSION FOR DR JONES by Lilian Darcy
Southshore - No.1 of 4

Dr Harry Jones is sure it's a mistake having Rebecca Irwin work in the practice. Despite the raging attraction between her and Harry, Rebecca fought her corner!

BACHELOR CURE by Marion Lennox
Bachelor Doctors

Dr Tessa Westcott burst into Mike Llewellyn's life like a red-headed whirlwind. She said exactly what she thought, and turned his ordered world upside down. It couldn't last. But Mike had to admit, she lightened his life.

HOLDING THE BABY by Laura MacDonald

Lewis's sister was abroad and he was left holding the baby—literally! He *badly* needed help with the three children and asked Jo Henry to be nanny. In a family situation, Jo and Lewis became *vividly* aware of each other...

SEVENTH DAUGHTER by Gill Sanderson

Specialist registrar Dr James Owen was everything Dr Delyth Price ever wanted in a man. But Delyth had a gift not everyone understood. James seemed prepared to listen, if not to believe. Then she discovered his lighthearted side, and fell even deeper into love...

Available from 3rd September 1999

MILLS & BOON®

Next Month's Romance Titles

♡

Each month you can choose from a wide variety of romance novels from Mills & Boon®. Below are the new titles to look out for next month from the Presents...™ and Enchanted™ series.

Presents...™

A BOSS IN A MILLION	Helen Brooks
HAVING LEO'S CHILD	Emma Darcy
THE BABY DEAL	Alison Kelly
THE SEDUCTION BUSINESS	Charlotte Lamb
THE WEDDING-NIGHT AFFAIR	Miranda Lee
REFORM OF THE PLAYBOY	Mary Lyons
MORE THAN A MISTRESS	Sandra Marton
THE MARRIAGE EXPERIMENT	Catherine Spencer

Enchanted™

TYCOON FOR HIRE	Lucy Gordon
MARRYING MR RIGHT	Carolyn Greene
THE WEDDING COUNTDOWN	Barbara Hannay
THE BOSS AND THE PLAIN JAYNE BRIDE	Heather MacAllister
THE RELUCTANT GROOM	Emma Richmond
READY, SET...BABY	Christie Ridgway
THE ONE-WEEK MARRIAGE	Renee Roszel
UNDERCOVER BABY	Rebecca Winters

On sale from 3rd September 1999

H1 9908

Available at most branches of WH Smith, Tesco, Asda, Martins, Borders, Easons, Volume One/James Thin and most good paperback bookshops

Spoil yourself next month
with these four novels from

TEMPTATION

MACKENZIE'S WOMAN by JoAnn Ross

Bachelor Auction

Kate Campbell had to persuade Alec Mackenzie to take part in a
charity bachelor auction. This rugged adventurer would have
women bidding millions for an hour of his time. Trouble was,
Alec wasn't really a bachelor. Though nobody knew it—he was
married to Kate!

A PRIVATE EYEFUL by Ruth Jean Dale

Hero for Hire

Nick Charles was a bodyguard on a vital assignment. But no one
had yet told him exactly what that assignment was! So he was
hanging around a luxury resort, waiting… Then along came
luscious Cory Leblanc and Nick just knew she was a prime
candidate—for *something*…

PRIVATE LESSONS by Julie Elizabeth Leto

Blaze

'Harley' turned up on Grant Riordan's doorstep and sent his
libido skyrocketing. Hired as the 'entertainment' for a bachelor
party, she was dressed like an exotic dancer but had the eyes of
an innocent. Unfortunately, after a little accident, she didn't
have a clue who she was…

SEDUCING SYDNEY by Kathy Marks

Plain-Jane Sydney Stone was feeling seriously out of place in a
glamorous Las Vegas hotel, when she received a mysterious
note arranging a date—for that night! She was sure the message
must have been delivered to the wrong woman. But maybe
she'd just go and find out…

FREE!

2 Books
and a surprise gift!

We would like to take this opportunity to thank you for reading this Mills & Boon® book by offering you the chance to take TWO more specially selected titles from the Medical Romance™ series absolutely FREE! We're also making this offer to introduce you to the benefits of the Reader Service™—

- ★ FREE home delivery
- ★ FREE gifts and competitions
- ★ FREE monthly Newsletter
- ★ Books available before they're in the shops
- ★ Exclusive Reader Service discounts

Accepting these FREE books and gift places you under no obligation to buy; you may cancel at any time, even after receiving your free shipment. Simply complete your details below and return the entire page to the address below. *You don't even need a stamp!*

YES! Please send me 2 free Medical Romance books and a surprise gift. I understand that unless you hear from me, I will receive 4 superb new titles every month for just £2.40 each, postage and packing free. I am under no obligation to purchase any books and may cancel my subscription at any time. The free books and gift will be mine to keep in any case.

M9EB

Ms/Mrs/Miss/Mr ....Initials..
BLOCK CAPITALS PLEASE

Surname..

Address..

....

....Postcode ....

Send this whole page to:
THE READER SERVICE, FREEPOST CN81, CROYDON, CR9 3WZ
(Eire readers please send coupon to: P.O. BOX 4546, KILCOCK, COUNTY KILDARE)

Offer not valid to current Reader Service subscribers to this series. We reserve the right to refuse an application and applicants must be aged 18 years or over. Only one application per household. Terms and prices subject to change without notice. Offer expires 29th February 2000. As a result of this application, you may receive further offers from Harlequin Mills & Boon and other carefully selected companies. If you would prefer not to share in this opportunity please write to The Data Manager at the address above.

Mills & Boon is a registered trademark owned by Harlequin Mills & Boon Limited.
Medical Romance is being used as a trademark.

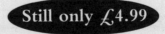